What You Long For

Short Stories by
Anne Clinard Barnhill

Mint Hill Books
Main Street Rag Publishing Company
Charlotte, North Carolina

Copyright © 2009 Anne Clinard Barnhill

Cover art: Adam Barnhill, a Raleigh, NC artist.
Author photo by Frank Barnhill.

Acknowledgements:

> *Grow Old Along With Me*: "Washing Helen's Hair"
> *Antietam Review*: "The Quilting Bee"
> *Cities and Roads*: "Final Frontier"
> *At Home in the Land of Oz*: "Visiting Jackie"
>   (as a chapter of memoir)
> *The Main Street Rag 2008 Short Fiction Anthology: Big Water*: "At Sea"
> *Mt. Olive Review*: "Kings and Damsels"
> *Racing Home: New Stories by Award-Winning NC Writers*: "Namesake"
> *Caprice*: "Lucy and Ethel"
> *Bare Root Review*: "Confessions of a Fat Woman"
> *Lonzie's Fried Chicken*: "Some Nameless Thing"
> *Generation to Generation*: "The Swing"

Library of Congress Control Number: 2009921587

ISBN 13: 978-1-59948-164-7

Produced in the United States of America

Main Street Rag
PO Box 690100
Charlotte, NC 28227
www.MainStreetRag.com

for my family

CONTENTS

Washing Helen's Hair.. 1
The Quilting Bee 8
Final Frontier . .. .26
Visiting Jackie 36
A Telephone Ministry.. 52
Kings and Damsels 65
Produce.. 75
Dickhead 87
Namesake. 92
Lucy and Ethel.. 105
Confessions of a Fat Woman 112
Where There's Smoke 131
Some Nameless Thing 144
The Perfect Pair. 152
Opal.. 168
The Swing. 182

What You Long For   v

WASHING HELEN'S HAIR

Helen kneels on the oak stool in front of the bathroom sink. Her knees, lumpy with arthritis, hit the faded red cushion with a soft thud. She caresses the familiar grain of the wooden legs, feels the varnish and where it's thinned in spots. The stool is hers, made for her years ago. She smiles.

Silly old thing, she mutters to herself. Ashamed now to let him see how you struggle into position. Almost dizzy, she rests her head on the cold rim of enamel.

"I'm ready, Lon. Waiting." Her voice cracks, not from emotion but from the strain of yelling for him to come to her. He's on the back porch, shucking corn from the garden. He planted only one patch this year after she refused to freeze the surplus. She's tired of his garden, tired of the peeling, boiling, cutting, chopping. She needs rest.

"I'm starting without you," she calls, turning on the faucet, letting the water run until it's warm. This resting on her knees isn't easy as it used to be. But she'd rather feel her feet go numb and walk on prickles than to give up her hair day. Twice a week, without fail. From what feels like the beginning of time, Alonzo has shampooed her. She cannot give it up.

What You Long For   1

She listens for his step, then turns the water on hard. He'll hear that, certainly. Lon could sense waste even with his bad ears. He might not pay attention to her voice, but he'll high-step it into the house to see why she's run so much water.

Sure enough, the slow gallumph of his steady stride up the hall vibrates the floor. She raises her head and spies him in the mirror, watches as he ambles towards her. His face is tanned from hours spent in the yard, digging roots, poking his fingers in to test the soil. He puts his old felt hat on the hall dresser, then heads to the bathroom. She notices how his back is now shaped like the curved needle her papa used to stitch jagged cuts on animals, sometimes people.

Lon wears his old white linen jacket, a Sunday morning uniform of years gone by. The collar, too worn now for church, circles his thin neck.. Helen doesn't like the way it looks, but he insists on gardening in it, though Helen laughs, calls him the ice cream man. He chuckles back at her in his gruff way. Last May, he bought a new suit, beige this time, for his churchgoing.

He rings her waist with his ropy arms.

"Had to finish the corn." His hair, sparse, streaks across his pate in thin pencil lines. Yet, Helen thinks he still cuts a fine figure, his large, veiny hands hanging at his sides. Her heart beats faster as she watches him in the mirror.

"About time." She fusses at him, not really meaning it, knowing he's used to her tart remarks.

"Water hot enough?" Alonzo tests it with his fingers, then bends around her to wash his hands with Ivory soap.

"Just right." Helen searches his reflection, looking for any corn worms that might have strayed onto him. She does hate a worm.

"Ain't any on me, missy. I got em all." He unbuttons her collar, then pulls down the zipper on her dress. She lets the front drop to her waist. He slides the straps off her shoulders so that he can touch her.

Anne Clinard Barnhill

She feels his rough fingers kneading the back of her neck, gently, always gently. Her shoulders, the back part of her head, midway down her spine. He continues to massage the dimpled skin until he hears her 'ah', his signal to take down her hair from the French twist at the nape of her neck. Carefully, he removes each fancy comb, then gingerly loosens the hairpins. Helen loves the free fall of the bun, the sudden lightness.

"I'm tender-headed." She makes a face at him in the mirror and watches his brown eyes crinkle with fond exasperation.

"I know, missy, I know." Her grey curls fall and cover his hands. The strands wind through his fingers. The hair, stiff and wiry, is the color of pewter. Helen sees his face change and imagines he's remembering how blond her hair used to be. And how soft.

She hands him her brush made of pig bristles and holds her head straight as he combs through the long rope of her hair.

"Still a pretty sight." Lon bends over, buries his face in her hair, its odor sweet and fresh like warm milk in a pail, the kind he used to carry up from the barn when he was a boy. He's told her this before, many times, confessed his love for her smell. She slowly leans her head over the sink. He begins to wet her hair, cupping his hand under the faucet, then pouring the warm water onto her scalp.

"Feels so good." Helen likes the weight of the water pulling her. Without him to hold her, she thinks she might spin down the drain, as in that silly nursery rhyme. Lon's fingers support her head with one hand as he begins to make whorls with the other.

"Still doing it, ain't we?" There it is, the reference to their agreement, the hard-won solution to their biggest problem in these late days of their marriage. Helen had feared rest homes all her life. And the older she grew, the more her terror seized her. Lon, however, liked the idea of being taken care of, the final relaxing a home would allow. For months they'd argued. Until they struck their bargain. They'd stay in their own home for as long as Alonzo could wash Helen's hair. If either became too ill or too stiff or just too tired, they'd move.

So far, their arrangement was working.

Helen smells strawberries when Lon opens the shampoo bottle. He surprises her with a new brand every so often, and she likes the changes, loves to think of him at the grocery store, poring over the different kinds, deciding which one she might enjoy.

He begins to hum. Helen hears him in the garden in the early morning, then on Sunday mornings before church. "When The Roll Is Called Up Yonder," one of the old-timey hymns from their youth.

He hummed the first time he washed her hair, not a hymn, though. Instead, it was that Steven Foster ditty about the girl with the long hair. She remembers how embarrassed she'd been, a girl barely fifteen, him, a man of twenty-six. They'd married in 1933 with little more than a suitcase of clothes to move into the hotel room they'd let from old Mrs. Abernathy. Helen laughs.

"What's so funny?" He scrubs her head, cleaning it good and hard, the way she likes. She wonders if he thinks it peculiar that she enjoys a rough scrubbing, yet she can't stand the slightest pulling of her hair.

"Oh nothing. I just thought about how scared I was of you back when we first got married." She places her hands on her thighs and pinches to get some feeling there. Not ready for him to stop, she hopes to delay the inevitable numbness. She won't let these old legs of hers force her into a home. She knows she ought to mention her pain, admit how she hurts for hours after the hair wash. She's promised to be honest with him, yet she can't bring herself to talk about the aches that follow her to bed.

Anne Clinard Barnhill

"Scared of me?" He's always been so slow and easy, she wonders if he's known this for all time.

"Yep. Especially on our wedding night. And when you wanted to bathe me and wash my hair, I didn't know what to do. Mama hadn't led me to expect anything like that." Helen grins. Thinking back takes her mind off the pain creeping into her legs.

She could see him as he was then, a tall, gangly man with dark curly hair and a black moustache. He was strong, able to heave bales of hay easily. His strength frightened her, but at the same time, excited her in a way she didn't understand. Before their marriage, he'd kissed her a few times. Pulled her to him, his breath fierce on her cheek, his hands and arms hard, nothing like her own limbs. Always, her body tensed against him, resistant, afraid.

She'd made up her mind to live through the wedding night, no matter what it took. After a fine dinner at the hotel and a stroll along the city street, she'd excused herself to the bath. She would at least be clean.

She'd been sitting on the edge of the clawfoot tub for a long time. Finally, she decided to get on with it. Her fingers were poised above her head, ready to take down her hair. She felt his strong hands on hers as she reached for the combs.

"Let me help you." He removed them, then ran his thick fingers through her hair, easing out the snarls. She'd felt the familiar bunching of her muscles, her whole body stiffening, preparing for his touch.

"My scalp is real tender." Her voice barely left her throat.

"I won't hurt you." She realized she stood before him in the light, wearing only her undergarments. A hot blush started across her chest.

"You'll strain your back leaning across the tub like that. We'll wash your hair in the sink, then I'll run your bath water. I'll get a chair." He raised her up, brushed the hair

What You Long For

away from her face. While he went for the chair, she wanted to slip into her robe, the one she'd embroidered for their honeymoon. But she just stood, her bare feet against the cool linoleum.

"This'll be a lot easier. Sit down and lean over the sink. That's it." With her head back to him, she felt her neck bend, thin as a dove's. She let him take the weight of her skull into his hands. First, he stroked her crown, then began to moisten her hair.

"Your hair's the first thing I noticed about you, missy. Yellow and shimmering in the sunlight." Lon had never been a sweet-talker. But now his voice was soft, easy. She relaxed into it.

Soon, her head full of suds, he'd raised her to a sitting position and piled her hair in funny shapes on top of her head. They'd laughed at the 'hairdos', a long soapy spike, a blob with a curl at the tip.

Later, clean from her bath, her hair slightly damp, he'd taken her to their bed.

Her knees ache and pop. She runs her hand across her outer thighs, no longer smooth and pearly, but speckled with blue splotches. Her golden hair now the dull color of storm clouds.

"Tired?" He's already rinsed her and now holds a large yellow towel slung across his forearm. Her special towel, her favorite color.

"Yes. My legs are numb as rubber and my feet have gone plumb to sleep." She doesn't mention the pain across her shoulder blades.

"We'll manage, missy." He helps her up and smiles at her in the mirror.

Helen catches his hands as he starts to wrap her head in the towel. They are rough hands, familiar. Age spots, brown and ragged, ride the veins. These are hands she can trust.

She brings the calloused fingers to her mouth and kisses them, her dry lips leaving only a hint of moisture behind.
"Thank you." She whispers, not knowing whether he hears her.

He gives no reply, just pats her shoulder and leads her to the overstuffed chair on the back porch where he will towel-dry her hair, the drying faster there in the sun. Helen allows herself to be led, her hand in his. She sinks back into the chair. He lifts her feet, one at a time, onto the hammock, rubs them for a moment until they are buzzing with warmth. Then he begins to comb her damp hair, carefully, so as not to pull a single strand.

THE QUILTING BEE

When I's a little girl, my mama used to take me to Ole Nearl's once every month when the moon was full. Women from miles around would go. She was so old by then that long, white hairs sprouted on her chin, and her voice scratched against itself like a sow at eating time. Why, her hands was like claws, and when she went to hug you, you felt hot and cold at the same time. Nearl was the best quilter in Hell's Holler.

I was usually the only child at Nearl's, except for little babies on the breast. They let me come along because of my ears—I could hear the whir of a bird's wing, the settling of the frogs way down under the frozen ground. I could hear the heartbeat of the bear in his slumber and the low snarl of a raccoon in the backyard. I was good for something—I could let them know if any of the menfolk were snooping around.

We'd gather in Nearl's front room around the quilting rack. Nearl'd make us a big, cozy fire, and together we'd stitch slow, tiny seams onto the bits of multi-colored cloth. And while we sewed, one of the women would tell a tale.

Every kind of woman sat around that circle. There was Teacall, the preacher woman whose pride and joy was a quilt she'd sewn with her mother, Tree of Life; and Lil Sis, who made the best biscuits, light and airy with a hint of cinnamon. Sis told stories that reached back, back to the beginnings of the hills themselves. She knew every member of her family, all the way to Eve. Her favorite was pattern was Grandma's Dream, and she'd made one for each of her seven children.

There was Curly Shirley, a strumpet who told tales on the men in the valley. Shirley knew the size of every pecker from here to Tennessee. She made herself a quilt called Honeycomb. And there was Dotty, who grew up in a chicken coop and never stopped talking. She rose in the morning chattering as if she'd never slept a wink. I've heard her say things to herself in the aisles of the general store; I've heard her mumble to the preacher when she didn't agree with him; I've heard her argue with the squirrels, and one time I heard her fight with the rafters in her attic. She yackety-yacks to stars, the sun and moon, the titmouse in the maple tree.

When the menfolk come to get their women after about seven days, they'd find Dotty still a-going, though the only woman left to hear her was Ole Nearl, half-asleep after drinking her spring tonic. The Honey Bees, that's what the women called themselves (and Nearl was the Queen, no one ever questioned that) made a crazy quilt for old Dotty and every meeting Dotty wraps herself in the bright patches of velvets and silks.

My favorite was the lady the other women called Mouse. She was small-boned with dark hair and cool, green eyes. Mouse didn't talk much, just slowly pulled her needle up and through the quilt. Sometimes she'd smile at a joke, but, for the most part, Mouse was quiet.

One night, when the wind was especially still on the mountain, Ole Nearl said, "Mouse, you been coming up here since you got your first blood. And you ain't never told one tale. This is your night, Miss Mousie. We ain't a-waiting no more."

I watched Mouse turn fiery red. Part of me felt sorry for her, but then part wanted to hear her speak. Silence fell on the room and for once, even Dotty shut up. When the quiet got so heavy you could heap it up with a spoon, Mouse began:

Got me a gun, Mouse said. And then more silence. Still more. More.

Got me a gun and I can hit the eyeball off an eagle, she said. No one uttered a word. The room felt full of something, and I wanted to know what it was.

Got me a gun and the first time Junior Hopkins kissed me, I fired it at the top of his head and parted his wavy black hair, Mouse said. We all kept our silent vigil. Moments passed. The night couldn't have been quieter.

Got me a gun and I fell in love with Junior that night, a love that fit around me like a bunch of tight ropes, she said.

Dotty whispered, "Got me a gun." Soon the whole room took it up like a chant. Ole Nearl was a-singing it, my granny and the rest, a roomful of women saying, "Got me a gun." Over and over they repeated the words. Soon, Mouse stood up and said in a bold voice:

That Junior Hopkins, he made me love him. He got into my blood and bones. That Junior Hopkins laid claim to me, sure as if I was a mine of coal. That Junior Hopkins, oh that Junior Hopkins, he opened up my heart and sliced it like a pear. And when he was done with me, when he was done, he rode the rails to Baltimore, rode across the hills to Baltimore and left me here to die.

"Left me here to die," the women chanted. "Left me here to die."

So I gathered up my clothes, dresses starched and fresh. I took the road to Baltimore, walking my feet smooth. Sleeping in the rain, marching in the mud, eating and not eating, I walked my way to Baltimore.

"Walked my way to Baltimore," echoed the women.

And when I got there, when I got to Baltimore, I found him in a whorehouse. Found him a-laying with a red-haired woman, a skinny red-haired witch, Mouse said.

"Skinny red-haired witch," sighed the women.

So I got my trusty gun, and I aimed right at his chest. I steadied my hand and pulled that heavy trigger. He fell like a rock, dead at me feet. Just dead at my feet.

"Dead, dead, dead at my feet," whispered the women.

That was twenty years ago, and I never told a word. Sometimes I hear him call me when the night is slow and dark. Hear him call my name soft and tender, him calling and me not answering, him calling my name, just calling my name. Mouse shivered and pulled her Love and Marriage quilt around her shoulders.

"Calling, calling my name," the women said softly until the room again grew silent.

After a long pause, Mouse sat down like on cue. Ole Nearl smiled at her and said, "Mighty good tale, Miss Mousie. You done real fine."

I watched as the women stared at their needles, their eyes steady on the stitches. Each patch of cloth was fitted to the next by tiny, tight seams, and as I looked at each woman, her face told me something different. My eyes fell on Curly Shirley. Even though I was just a girl, I knew what she was. Granny had told me the wages of sin many a-time, and I could see the tired marks around Curly Shirley's mouth, the dull blue of her eyes. I'd heard Shirley's crazy stories before, and my belly hurt with laughing most nights when Shirley talked about men and peckers, peckers and men. While I was a-staring at her, Shirley began to speak:

Mine's a real Cinderella fairy tale, girls. I was five days old when my mama left me on the doorstep of the mining boss. Left me and never come back. Boss's wife, she took me in and raised me up with her two daughters. Treated me like I was lower than the coal in them mines. Made me wash clothes every Monday and hoe the garden after school. I washed dishes after supper and them girls did their homework and played with their dolls. I didn't ever get a doll, not even at Christmas time. My stocking would have a couple of apples in it, bruised ones. Old lady said my stocking had a big hole in it, so Santa couldn't put much in there. But them girls got enough for me and three other kids.

When I was seven, the Boss come to my little room off the back porch. It didn't have no heat in there, but I had a big blanket and slept with one of the pups that ran around the yard. I heard the Boss step easy out the back door and heard his soft slide to my room. Must have been in his stocking feet cause he didn't make any noise like the clomp, clomp he usually made when he walked. The door cracked open and I could see a sliver of moonlight shine across my bed. He was nothing but shadow.

He never spoke one word to me. He pulled off the covers and lifted up my nightgown. I didn't say nothing, just lay there still as I could be. He touched my legs and then he touched me all over my shivering body. I could hear him moaning and breathing ragged. Something warm fell on my legs, warm like rain. Then, he wiped it off of me real tender-like. I didn't say a word. He sat down beside me and told me in a gruff voice that I was going to get me a nice doll real soon. I'd get me a pretty doll with open-and- shut eyes. He told me not to tell anybody he'd come in here. He said if I could keep a secret real good, he'd bring me the prettiest doll he could find. Then he kissed me on the top of my head and left me out there, still shaking like a leaf in the wind.

I got that doll on his next payday. I got a whole roomful of dolls by the time I left that house, a whole roomful. I still got em. They're packed up in an old trunk. Packed up like all the babies I never had. One of these long winter nights, I'm gonna burn that old trunk. Burn up them babydolls, let em burn till their hair curls up and falls off. Burn them babies, all them soft-bodied, hard-faced babydolls.

This time, nobody laughed at Curly Shirley's story. I didn't know why she wanted to burn all them dolls. I sure wished I could have one.

Ole Nearl rose and shook her pinched up face at the women. "I believe it's time fer some homebrew, ladies.

What ye say?" When Nearl stood, she was bent over so far she looked like she was still sitting down. I was taller than she was—me just a girl.

"That's a good idea, Miz Nearl," Dotty said. "I ain't had any of your homebrew since the last time I come a-quilting. I've always love the way you make that brew, Nearl. When you gonna give me that recipe? Indeed, I'd like to give it a try. My old man tries to make the stuff, but his comes out rough. Ain't a bit smooth, like yers. How you do it, Miz Nearl? You gonna share that secret?" Dotty took Ole Nearl's arm and helped her into the kitchen. I could hear Dotty a-jabbering in there the whole time, like the woodpeckers in spring. Curly Shirley hadn't said a word since she told her tale, but the other women were patting her shoulder and touching her on the hair, real kind, real gentle-like. My granny was one of them that hugged Shirley and kissed her on her cheek. Her story wasn't all that great, if you ask me.

Dotty came from the kitchen carrying a tray of glasses filled with an amber-colored something, except for one glass of milk I knew was mine. The tray was covered with a small Friendship Quilt the Bees had made for Ole Nearl, each piece of fabric hooked up with the next.

"Here's one fer you, little 'un. And here's fer the real women. Now, who's a-gonna start up another story? Who's a-gonna tell a tale? Ole Nearl be in here in jest a minute. Had to use the slop jar on the back porch. Law, I thank the Lord fer slop jars. Ain't it awful to go to the outhouse late at night? Why, I jest imagine there's thangs in them woods, thangs a body ought never to see. I said to my husband just the other day, Honey, I said, ain't a slop jar a great thang? And I specially like em when they got them little pink flowers on em, like they was something special. Yes, I said to him, a slop jar is a gift from God. But he didn't say a word, jest look at me funny. Have some of these oatmeal cookies with yer brew. They's got raisins in em," Dotty rambled on. She passed the plate and took a cookie for herself.

What You Long For

She took a bite and that shut her up. Ole Nearl shuffled back to her chair and picked up her needle to start a-quilting again. Nearl gave Dotty a hard glance, and Dotty said no more.

"Ain't heard from you in quite a spell, Teacall. Why don't ye tell us a good one?" Nearl said in her scratched-out voice. The murmurs of the sewing women grew silent, and everyone waited fer Teacall to begin. I didn't like her stories because they scared me to death—all about devils and demons and wickedness.

Reckon I got one in me. Yet and still, I ain't got em like I used to. Why, when I was a young gal, them stories would come like rolling thunder. They'd pass through my brain, a strong wind like to take my breath sometimes. The Lord was a-prophesizing in them days. Now, stories don't come but once or twice a year, and they kindly trickle in, one little word at a time. But here's one I been a-thinking about—

Long time ago when the mines was just dug and the mining companies bought out all the mineral rights, there was a feud twixt the miners and the bosses. The big boss was a bear of a man, and, as I recall, nobody tween here and Tennessee could whip him. The miners ain't got no army, ain't got nothing but clubs and such, but the bosses had rifles and guns. The miners numbered around a hundred to the bosses' twenty-some. But they had them guns and was holed up in the courthouse with its rock walls and high towers.

The fighting went on fer a week with miners getting shot and kilt every day. Finally, the Boss said he'd fight any man the miners sent out to him, fight him fair and square. Now, the miners didn't know of anybody who could best the Bossman. He was tall as a hemlock and meaner than a slag-pile cat. The miners talked and drew straws, and finally, a young feller named Brady turned up with the short end of the stick. Now Brady wasn't much more than a boy, really, but he could trap and hunt with the best of em. He was peculiar in a way, though. He was a gospel singer and had a voice that could lift ye to heaven. I'd hear him a-singing on his way to work way back when I's a girl. He knew how to throw a lump of coal and knock tin cans off a fence at fifty paces. He was handsome and shapely, and he marched out to meet the Boss brave as a rooster. In each hand he held a nugget of coal, shiny and hard and black as tar. The Boss laughed right out loud when he saw Brady, like to give himself a belly ache.

Then, he raised up his arm and started toward Brady with killing in his eyes. Brady stood his ground, and when the Boss moved into range, Brady let fly with them two rocks and each one a-hit the Boss square between the eyes. Boss fell over dead as any possum. The miners screamed and hollered, and that very day, they elected Brady to be their new boss, and he was one of the best ones to ever run the mines in these here mountains.

Teacall stopped, took a sip of her brew, nibbled a little bit of cookie, then continued:

Brady grew rich, but he never quit his church, and he kept on a-singing. The years was good to him, and he married, started a family. One night, he was outside a-looking off his big front porch over the roofs of the town, feeling contented, satisfied. He could see inside the window of the small house across the field from him. He owned that house, but rented it out, had his lawyer do all the collecting and lease mess. He didn't even know who came and went in that little house.

He saw her through the window, and she was unlike any woman he'd known. He watched as she slipped out of her dress and climbed into the big iron bed, her long dark hair a-tumble. He was struck dumb, couldn't move. Right then, he began to build a temple to that woman in his heart.

Asked his lawyer who she was, found out she was married to a man who worked in his coal mines. Brady sent for that woman one night while her old man was a-working third shift. He met her out at the barn and went to work on her. It was like he was in the grip of some dream, like he'd done left this world and gone to a place he hadn't known existed. He loved her like a storm, all thunder and roiling clouds.

After three weeks, Brady sent her husband down in Century Number Two, the oldest mine in the mountain. Weren't safe and Brady knew it. The mine caved in and killed the husband. It was murder. Everybody said so. But couldn't prove nothing. Brady and the woman went on, but he never sang no more. And after the baby come, ain't nothing left of whatever held him so. And he never sang no more, never no more.

The women shook their heads. Dotty was opening her mouth to say something when I heard a sigh from outside.

"Shhh. Something's a-coming," I whispered. The women got so still I wasn't sure they was a-breathing. I listened hard. I could hear the wind, a little breeze singing. I could hear the raccoons in the back yard rummaging. And I could hear the sound of men trying to be real quiet.

"They's men outside," I said.

"Why can't they leave us alone?" Dotty whispered.

"Hush!" said Ole Nearl. Slow as a slug crawling on sand, Ole Nearl got up and hobbled to the door where she kept her rifle. She grabbed the gun and opened the door just enough to stick the tip of the rifle outside. She pulled the trigger and fell back into Dotty's waiting arms.

"Damn, they's a-shooting at us," one of the men said.

"Witches!" yelled another.

"Can't believe my mama'd shoot me. My sweet old mama?" yet another hollered.

"Run, boys, run!"

The sound of the scurrying men tickled the women inside, but they didn't laugh, though Dotty had to put her hand over her mouth to keep from it. I could hear them men tripping over roots and slipping down trails of pebbles. A-cussing and a-fussing, they high-tailed it down the mountain.

"They keep a-trying, don't they?" said Ole Nearl. "Won't never leave us alone. We work day and night, bear their bodies and their babies. And when we take off our time each month, they can't stand it. Got to know what we're up to, got to get us back in our houses a-cooking and a-cleaning. Well, they won't be back." Nearl put the gun back in its place and leaned against the Drunkard's Path that was folded and a-lying on the back of her rocker. The women's bodies could be heard moving and shifting as their needles dug in and out of the quilt they were working on.

"Let's hear another story. How about you, Lil Sis?" said Ole Nearl.

Lil Sis cleared her throat all stopped up with her holding her breath while the men were outside. She threaded her needle and commenced to sewing while she talked. The other women did the same.

Well, there once was a woman who refused to get married. This happened a long time ago, back when every girlchild in these mountains got hitched when they was about fourteen. But this woman, Lucille was her name, she didn't want nothing to do with men. Couldn't stand em. Funny thing was, though, she dressed just like a man. Wore workboots and overalls, wool shirts and longjohns. She worked hard on her little farm raising goats and selling the cheese and milk to nursing mothers whose milk had gone bad. She weren't an ugly-looking woman. She was strong and lean, tall and had long, golden hair she kept up under her hat. She was kind to children and helpful to their mamas, but she had no truck with men.

One day down at the general store, a bunch of young bulls watched her load up her wagon with grain and feed. After she drove away, Moose, the biggest young man in the valley said, 'I'm gonna marry Lucille. By jingles, she's a fine woman.' The men laughed.

'She ain't gonna marry you, Moose. She don't like men. She's one of them sufferers. Probably thinks women ought to vote,' said Cole, a skinny runt of a man with bright orange hair.

'We'll see, boys. We'll just see,' said Moose.

So Moose started a-courting Lucille. He come to her cabin with a handful of wildflowers, but she wouldn't even let him on

What You Long For

the porch. He brought a jar full of honey in the comb, but she shot at him when he set foot in the yard. He dropped that honey and ran down the mountain faster than a dog turn-tails when he spies a skunk. Next, he sent Cole with a bag of seed fer planting the next spring. Cole was too scairt to get close to the house, so he just left the bag next to the barn door and ran. Moose didn't bother sending Cole after that.

It plumb drove Moose crazy that Lucille didn't want him. He figured he was doing her a favor courting her when she was nigh onto twenty. He knew she'd be a-wanting younguns, and he figured he was the man to give em to her. But still, he couldn't get close enough to holler at her, much less love her.

He took to spying on her whenever he could. On Sundays, he'd watch from behind a big boulder near her house, stare at her while she milked her goats and put up hay. He loved the form of her, long lanky curves set nice against the evening sky. He was bent to win her somehow, but he couldn't figure out how.

Then it hit him. Every Saturday, Lucille hiked up to the top of the mountain where she gathered the leaves of the blackberry bush fer tea and hunted fer ginseng. He'd followed her up there a few times, watching how careful she was searching out the earth fer its goodness. She'd throw off her cap and her hair would fly out like wings. Oh, how he wanted to grab it in his fists and feel the silkiness of it. Sometimes, he could hear her a-singing or a-whistling, and it made his heart grow big. He loved Lucille and by damn, he'd have her.

His plan was to follow her up to the mountain top and then, just take her. He'd put a bun in her oven and then she'd have to say yes. No woman would live with the shame of a baby ill-got. No woman would live ruint. Moose smiled when he thought about it. Since she was too stubborn to know what was good for her, he'd show her. He'd show her what she'd been a-missing.

That next Saturday, Moose done just what he planned. Nobody raised an eyebrow when he explained in town how he'd broke his arm a-falling out of a tree. He might have a broken arm, but, by God, he'd had Lucille, too. Tearing at him, clawing him, kicking and shoving him in every soft spot he had—by God, he'd finally got her soft spot.

"That low-down man," said Dotty.

"Uh huh," said the other women.

"That ain't the end of the story, ladies. It gets worse," said Lil Sis.

"Nothing worse than that," said Dotty.

"Just listen," said Lil Sis.

Lucille didn't come into town fer a long time after what Moose done to her. She lay low through the winter and come spring she finally rode in fer supplies. With her, she had a bundle of joy. She drove her buggy straight up to the general store, her babe slung across her back like a papoose, and strode up the steps, walking right in front of Moose and a bunch of them young fellers. She never gave them a look, but kept her eyes straight ahead, done her business, then returned to her wagon.

'Don't you need a daddy fer that baby?' Moose yelled to her. He was amazed how she looked no different after having the baby. If anything, she looked prettier than ever, softer in a way that made him want to claim her and her baby. The crowd of young men whistled and made strange grunting sounds. Lucille stepped down off the wagon, faced those boys.

'My baby's daddy wasn't nothing but a one-minute wonder,' she said. 'And if I ever see the bastard again, I'll cut his heart out.' Then Lucille turned and climbed in her wagon. The men on the porch were quiet. Something in Lucille's voice had chilled their blood.

Lucille named her baby Ishmael, and she loved him with all the love that was in her. She never held his daddy against him. Instead, she turned her mind to ways of making enough money to buy little Ishmael the things he needed. She started raising chickens and sold the eggs along with her goat's milk and cheese. She was smart with a dollar and knew how to save and scrimp along. Why, she went fer eighteen years without a new dress while Ishmael had crisp new shirts from the Wish Book and shiny boots too.

When Ishmael was about three years old, the people in town found Moose dead in the woods. Looked like he'd met up with a bear, had claw marks all over his face and arms. Funny thing was, his heart was tore clean out of his chest. Of course, nobody thought about Lucille a-doing the deed cause there was bear tracks all in the mud. But it did make folks go to church regular fer a while.

From that time on, Lucille became more and more important to the town. Eggs, milk, cheese, and in the summer the biggest, juiciest tomatoes and nicest squash. Blackberries and blackberry tea, ginseng fer the men and raspberries fer the women. These things came from Lucille. And people grew to respect Lucille, her strong arms and the way she took care of herself and Ishmael.

"Well, there's a good end to that one," said Dotty. "Fire's a getting a little thin. Reckon I'll bring in more wood from the porch, if that's all right with you, Nearl." Dotty maneuvered her way out the door, carrying on the conversation, though we couldn't hear her from outside, except fer me. I could hear anything. But she didn't make much sense, a-talking about wood and how much she loved a good wood pile.

"This ought to do fer a spell. I think we ought to be thankful fer wood, ladies. Why, chopping it keeps us strong and burning it keeps us warm. Well, chopping it warms us some too, I reckon. And the smell is … ."

"Dotty. Let Lil Sis finish her story," said Ole Nearl in that rasp of hers.

"You mean it ain't no happy ending?" Dotty asked.

"No. No happy ending," said Lil Sis. "Here's what happened:

Ishmael grew into a strong, handsome young man. He had his daddy's strength and his mama's good looks. Even though Lucille taught the boy everything she knew about working the farm, he didn't take to it. He'd rather spend his nights a-drinking at the general store with the other boys. This scared Lucille and she wondered just how much of his daddy Ishmael had in him. She read him the Bible, she talked to him about everything good in the world, she told him how she loved him. Didn't do no good.

One morning Lucille went to wake Ishmael, and he weren't there. His clothes and all his gear was gone. Lucille let out a wail like the scream of a wild cat, hitched up her buggy, and drove like hell to town. But Ishmael weren't there. Nobody'd seen him.

Lucille returned home and sat down in her porch rocker. I don't know how long she sat there, just a-waiting fer him to come home. But she never heard from him again. And the next time I saw her, her golden hair had all turned white. That's the truth.

The women shook their heads and commenced sewing. Fer a long time, nobody said a word. It was past midnight and I could hear the clouds rolling by in the night sky. The stories were a-winding down, and, though I knew I had no business doing it, I spoke up.

"Why don't you give Dotty a turn? She ain't told one yet," I jammered.

Ole Nearl fixed her eyes on me and my skin quivered.

"Dotty ain't got no stories left. Why do you think she talks so much, child? She ain't got no stories in her, but she loves to listen. That dear old gal loves to listen," Ole Nearl said. She leaned over to pat Dotty's arm.

I didn't say another word, but I wondered why Dotty didn't have any stories left. How could a person run out of stories? The more I thought about it, the more confused I got. Why, if you didn't have a story left, were you still alive? Did you have a regular brain? Everybody's got lots of stories. Don't they? What does it mean when somebody ain't?

"You tell us one, Nearl," Dotty said. "I love yers the best. Please, the night's almost gone. Tell us one, Nearl. Come on. Tell us how you made yer first quilt—Too Little Too Late."

"I done told that one. I'll tell the one about my old man and his come-uppance," Ole Nearl said.

My old man, Jake, lasted about seventy years, most of em good. We hitched up when I's fifteen, and Jake was seventeen. Back in them days, he was a handsome man. Not too tall, I never did cotton to a tall man, with well-made hands and a broad chest. Oh, I loved him the way only a fifteen-year-old girl can love—with her whole

What You Long For

heart. He loved me too. We had five babies in five years and I was busy with feeding and washing and diapering all them children. That's when Jake started his cheating.

Now, some women'll say a man can't help hisself when it comes to cheating. And they'll turn their head, look the other way. And some women just do as the man does—start cheating themselves. Others'll shrivel up and die inside, but keep doing the regular outside stuff. Others might leave. But what I did was cure the problem at the ROOT."

"Whew! The ROOT!" yelled the women, just a-laughing and a-cackling. I didn't know what was so funny, but I giggled just the same like I was one of them.

Now ladies, you know how sensitive a man is about the ROOT. And I was mad as a wet hen that Jake done me that way. He was shucking around over at wild Melinda's like he was a free man. And me, a-waiting fer his sorry ass back home with them five younguns. Ole Nearl's voice grew stronger and smoother with every word.

Well, I figured out that the only way to fix Jake was to teach him a lesson. I wasn't the kind of woman to play turn-about with some other fellow. That woulda been against my religion. But what I thought of was better.

Late one night while Jake was over at Melinda's, I gathered me some cayenne peppers than had been drying in the attic. I started boiling them to make a strong brew. I added oil of peppermint and some eucalyptus salve, plus some of my mama's special slime fer burning the poison ivy off. I mixed it up real good. That stuff would like to take the skin off a pig.

Jake come in after midnight, all worn out. I was a-waiting fer him in my see-through nightie, the one he liked so much. I might have born five children, but I was only twenty and still had my figure. I could get a rise out of Jake most any time I wanted. But I knew that now he'd have nothing left after seeing Melinda, and I knew he couldn't tell me why.

So, he come into the house, and there I stood, my hair all down around my shoulders.

Howdy, Jake,' I said soft and low. I hurried over to him and gave him a big hug, rubbed my boobies against him. Then I kissed him real good.

'What you doing up, Nearl? I figured you'd be sound asleep by now.' He shimmied out of his jacket and held me to him.

'Couldn't sleep, baby. Couldn't sleep without your love,' I said to him while I ran my hands over his hair. Then I kissed him again.

'It's too late tonight, honey. I'm worn out. Probably couldn't get the old plumbing to work, I'm so tired,' he said without one bit of guilt.

'I got something fer that,' I said. 'Go git in the bed and I'll bring it.' I knew he'd be curious, and his wanting to know would bring him where I wanted him. 'Take off yer britches and I'll be right there.' I kissed him again and ran my tongue down the side of his neck.

I went into the kitchen to get the salve, keeping the lid on so he couldn't smell what was a-coming. I could hear him in the bedroom taking off his boots and slipping his long johns off. I pulled my nightgown down over one shoulder so he could see my smooth white arms and the little rise of my breasts. Then I bit my lips a little so they'd be red and swollen.

I walked into the bedroom and Jake was already lying on his back with his hands crooked behind his head. He just smiled at me when I hopped up beside him. I started a-messing with him, but nothing happened. I did everything a woman can do in such a case, but, like I knew, nothing would work.

'What's the matter, baby? Don't you want me?' I asked, innocent as could be.

'Oh, that ain't it, Nearl. Naw, that ain't it at all. You're just amazing me right now, just amazing me. I .... I .... don't know what's wrong,' he lied.

'Well, let me try this salve my mama told me about. She gave it to me on our wedding day and told me someday I might have to use it. You just relax and close yer eyes, Jake.'

He did as I told him. I grabbed a handful of that stuff, and it started to burn my fingers and palm the minute I touched it. I didn't care. I didn't mind suffering to teach Jake a lesson. I rubbed it all over him, right up under his family jewels all the way to the tip of his pecker.

It took a minute fer the burning to start.

'Nearl, what the hell have you done?' he screamed.

'Not near what I'm gonna do if you ever go to Melinda's or to any other woman fer what you ought to be a-getting from me. You thought you was such a sly dog, a-lying and all, but I knew what you been up to. I'll always know, Jake,' I said.

'I'm on fire! I'm a-burning up! Do something, Nearl.'

'Nothing I can do. It'll quit in a while. Then you can ice it down,' I said calm as milk. I knew there'd be no permanent damage, just the pain.

'Ice! Get it now, Nearl. Get the damn ice now!' he yelled.

'Get it yourself! I left a bucket on the back porch—just stick yourself in there for a while—that'll cool you,' I said.

He ran through the kitchen and I heard the back door slam. I followed him and watched him lower his pecker into the bucket, his face full of relief.

'Remember, Jake, if you ever cheat on me again, it'll be worse. And I'll always find out. I got ways of knowing, Jake, ways you ain't even heard of.' I went to him and rubbed ice over him. Tears ran down his cheeks, and my sinuses were getting cleared up.

'I won't, Nearl. I won't never cheat again.'

And he didn't. He was the best husband a woman could ask fer after that. We was married over fifty years and I never had to use the salve again, not once.

"We all need some of that salve," said Dotty. "Hell, I could use some right now. My old man don't know the meaning of the word –'cleave only unto her.'"

I didn't think Nearl's story made a lot of sense. But the women just laughed and laughed, talking about roots and rods and heat. I was sleepy and felt my head dropping

Anne Clinard Barnhill

onto the pillow next to me. The women were finished fer that night, though they still had four nights to go before returning to the men in their lives. And more stories, always more stories to quilt by. They were working on a quilt they called Delectable Mountains. I thought they ought to design one called Tales and Tails, but nobody paid me any mind.

FINAL FRONTIER

Bernie hears voices in the shower, muffled sounds hovering at the edge of sense. The noise teases, promises, the way his mother's voice would rise and fall as she talked on the phone when he was a kid. He'd snuggle in his bedroom, quiet, pretending sleep. After a short while, the click, click, click of the rotary dial would prick his ears and he'd listen as his mother chatted with her best friend, Lucy. Bernie would strain to catch that one-sided conversation, to figure out what made his mother laugh her rare, tinkling laugh. He never discovered the secret and he remembers how he'd fall asleep with his mother's voice wrapped around him, a thick, warm coverlet of sound.

Now he hears something similar, something comforting yet strange, coming from the bath.

He leans into the spray of water. He thinks if he could just get a little closer, he'd understand it all. But the talk is too fuzzy, blurred so that the insides of the syllables run together. It's a guttural language, like Klingon.

At first Bernie figures the noise comes from the apartment next door. Or maybe Mrs. McCormick, his landlady, home early from work, sick—the cold season, after all. He steps out of the stall, dries himself, then dresses quickly. He can finish later, so long as he's clean by this afternoon when he's scheduled for work. He sticks his thin neck into the hall to check Mrs. McCormick's apartment door across the way, three doors down. She leaves a blue tag on the doorknob if she's available for complaints or payments. If she doesn't want to be disturbed, the red tag and an envelope hang from the knob, an invitation to pay or make suggestions about the building. Bernie has never bothered Mrs. McCormick, not even when her blue tag dangled in full view. Most things that break down, he fixes himself. Or he lives with the imperfection. The slow drip of his kitchen faucet is easily repaired but the stained ceiling from the leaky upstairs apartment gives him something to stare at, to figure on, while he watches "Jeopardy".

Mrs. McCormick isn't home. He sees the red square of cardboard bright as an emergency vehicle light against her white metal door. He sighs, his slightly curved back creating a hollow sound rather than the full healthy 'ah' of an extended chest. Bernie's back gets more stooped every year and he seems to shrink, like a huge weight is slowly grinding him deeper into the ground. He thinks of defying the law of gravity, imagines himself weightless in outer space, orbiting the moon in giant circles, his backbone free at last. It's one of his favorite fantasies and sometimes he forgets his hump until he's in the shower and catches the C-shape of himself in the bathroom mirror.

The harsh brnnggg of the telephone startles Bernie as he closes the door. He jumps. Skitterish as a mouse, his mother used to say. Bernie hasn't changed the old rotary phone since his mother died three years ago, though he's considered switching to touch-tone. The phone was hers really. She needed to keep up with her bridge club, the circle at church and Bernie's boss down at Davis Drugstore. When Bernie took sick with a rare flu bug, she'd call the pharmacy to explain his absence. Then she'd go into great detail about the way his illness rattled him.

"He's been up all night, Ned, with a fever and all morning with runny bowels. I'm keeping him on clear liquids. Yes, I will. Thanks so much." She'd clang down the phone so that a slight hum echoed in the apartment long after she'd quit talking. Bernie stayed in his bed whenever she called in for him. He couldn't stand hearing his symptoms discussed. But now, he wouldn't mind so much, wouldn't object to hearing her voice, a voice he could recognize and understand.

The phone blares again. He reaches for the receiver, his hands still shaking. Usually he can catch it before the second ring.

"Sure, Mr. Davis. I can come early. No problem. I'll just finish my shower. No big deal." Again Ned wants him to cover for the new guy. Called in sick, the second time this week. Bernie smiles, knows he's the best employee Ned's got—conscientious, courteous, and consistent. His mother's list of virtues for a working man.

Then Bernie remembers the shower, the strange sounds gurgling up from the pipes. His hands are still trembling and he tries to calm them by rubbing them together, an old trick from childhood.

He prepares for his bath, taking his time. He carefully lays out clean underwear and gets a white towel from the perfect stack in the closet. He takes off his clothes, folds the knit slacks over a hanger, then places the beige golf shirt on the same hanger. He feels sporty when he wears the new shirt. His pale skin reflects the dim bathroom bulb. He stands, shivering on the bath mat. For a moment he enjoys the soft furriness of the white rug.

Somehow, he can't make himself re-enter the stall. He's afraid of the voices. He decides to rely on his mother's method of keeping clean—the sponge bath.

He runs the sink full of warm water, soaps up his washcloth until it's frothy with the smell of Zest, and scrubs his private parts first. He loves the slippery feel of suds there. Then he rinses and moves on to his armpits. If he can keep these areas clean, he doesn't think anyone will suspect him of avoiding a real shower.

He washes his hair in the sink, bent over until the curve of his spine feels like the bones will surely break. He imagines scattered vertebra shooting across the linoleum, clanking against the tiles like steely marbles. He makes it all the way to the rinse without standing up. When he finally extends his spine as far as he can, soap oozes down his back, slick and shimmery as snail trails, until he can once again bend over the white enamel to rinse.

The trouble with hearing voices, Bernie decides as the warm water gushes over his almost bald crown, is that he can't understand what they are saying. This confusion over content makes Bernie feel like maybe he's losing his mind. What's the point of speaking if you can't be understood? Why bother?

Bernie towels his brown hair dry. It doesn't take long to soak water from the sparse hairs around the edge of his head. While he feels the rub of the scratchy towel across his pink skin, he wonders about those TV shows, the ones that explain psychic phenomena. Some people on the shows hear voices. Maybe Bernie's a psychic. Could be he's got some kind of radar tuned in on the universe. But those people on television can always understand what's being said. Bernie can't. He folds his towel, draws a straight line through his hair, parting the few strands perfectly.

For a moment he considers angels. He's always loved the idea of an angel—white, fluffy wings poised for flight, a pale gold halo. But it seems an angel wouldn't appear in one's shower, wouldn't want to catch one without his clothes. An angel would have more class.

Bernie puts on his work slacks and admires their crisp crease. He learned from his mother to press clothing as precisely as any dry cleaners. He buttons the starched collar of his white shirt and ties a perfect Windsor knot in a blue-striped tie. Bernie's always careful of his appearance, especially when he's on his way to the drug store. He splashes his face with Obsession for Men. Since his mother's death, he's had more money to spend on such items. Aftershave is one of his favorite splurges.

Bernie pokes his head out the back door that leads out to the small cement patio and notices storm clouds on the far horizon. He picks up the large black umbrella from its stand and heads for the store. He walks briskly, proud that he's a man with someplace important to go. He can see the big Davis Drugstore sign from the sidewalk and hurries. Once inside the store, he assumes his duties without delay.

"Good afternoon, Mrs. Bumphus. And how are you today?" Bernie knows all the pharmaceutical regulars by name and he usually can remember their refills. Mrs. Bumphus has arthritis and he knows she's in for her monthly supply of high-power Motrin.

"Can't complain. A woman of seventy-one has her share of aches and pains." Mrs. Bumphus is one of Bernie's special customers. He has seven "specials". Mrs. Bumphus is an avid "Jeopardy" fan and Bernie likes to discuss categories with her.

"Did you see our show last night? Wasn't that a weird draw. Who ever heard of 'proteins' as a category?" He stacks vitamins, placing each bottle in its perfect niche, while he waits for the pharmacist to fill her order.

"I didn't know a one. But I did okay in 'Presidents'" Mrs. Bumphus studies laxatives. It's not the first time and Bernie wishes he could suggest psyllium, but he doesn't know if her stomach would be up to it.

"Here you are. That's $15.95. And stay tuned to our old friend, Alex."

Bernie notices Ned out of the corner of his eye. In his white coat Ned looks so professional. Like he could never make a mistake. But he does sometimes. Bernie's caught some real bloopers and if it hadn't been for Bernie's careful eye, Ned might have been sued. But Ned never acknowledged Bernie's help and even after the third error, Bernie still couldn't call Ned 'Ned' to his face.

"Hurry up with those vitamins, Bernie. Ya don't have to alphabetize em, for Christ's sake. Just shelve em." Ned's tone is impatient, as usual. Bernie's hands begin to quiver, just slightly.

"Yes, Mr. Davis. Right away." Bernie continues to put them in order, but forces his hands to work more quickly. He's convinced the customers can find them more easily the way he organizes them.

The walk home is what Bernie needs after a tough day of keeping up with Ned. The welcoming streetlights beam warmth over him. He stops for a moment underneath the pulsing fluorescent and enjoys the familiar hum. He feels bathed in some kind of benevolent glow. He raises his face toward the light and hears a low rumble. The voices? Here? He can't move. Then he sees the approaching headlights of the city bus. He quickly drops his gaze and continues walking.

All evidence of rain is gone. In the dark, Bernie pretends he stands straight and tall, firm like Captain Kirk on Star Trek, the old version. It's his favorite TV show and he watches the reruns every night at 11:30 PM. He thinks about aliens, creatures different from humans, kinder and more advanced.

He almost wishes a space craft would zip along, hover over him letting light fall in a circle around him, then take him aboard. He'd love to go where no man has gone before. Be a hero. Save the world. Heck, save the galaxy.

Instead, a cloud moves over the half moon and Bernie fumbles with the lock on his apartment door. A hot shower would feel so good. But Bernie remembers the voices and settles for hot tea and a sponge bath instead.

The next morning Bernie gets up early. Today he's decided to take a shower, voices or not. He pours skim milk over his Wheaties, breakfast of champions. He watches as the tannish-brown flakes sink, heavy as soggy cardboard. He spoons them into his mouth, thin lips closing over the mouthful. His mother had a real thing about chewing silently, with one's mouth closed like a clamp. Then he notices a burp, burp, hiss coming from the coffee pot.

The noise isn't the usual hum. The electric pot, a resident of Bernie's kitchen since his boyhood, seems ready to give up the ghost, as his mother used to say. She'd received the tin contraption as a wedding present and Bernie saw no reason to get rid of it, even when the newfangled machines came out. He likes the gurgle of perking coffee.

But this sound, at first so familiar, has taken on a different quality. The bubbling is deeper and less rhythmic. Bernie sits, forgetting his cereal for the moment. The noise is hypnotic.

Suddenly, the kitchen is completely silent. Bernie shakes his head, then picks up his spoon for another bite of cereal. He hears a rumble that's so loud he can't figure where it's coming from. Then he remembers he's heard that noise before.

The toilet. The voices have moved to the commode. Bernie gets up quietly, then bends to pull off his slippers. He'll check this out in his bare feet in case there's some kind of overflow. He tiptoes toward the noise.

The sounds grow louder the closer Bernie gets, as if the entire building is vibrating from some deep inner place. By the time Bernie reaches the bathroom, his head is spinning and he feels light. He stands in front of the commode and peers in.

Nothing. Then he notices the water is moving. The sounds struggle up and Bernie listens. He strains to understand.

An idea hits him—one Einstein would have been proud of. Bernie rushes into his bedroom, shuffles through his bottom drawer, finds an old tape recorder and microphone. He checks the batteries the way his mother taught him, by touching the tip of his tongue to the top of the copper. He feels the familiar zing on his tastebuds, then heads back to the toilet.

He plops the microphone into the john, then flushes. The mike disappears for a moment, then returns almost to its original spot. Bernie reaches down to retrieve it. The mike doesn't move. It's stuck.

Bernie tries not to panic, but no matter how hard he tugs on the wire, the microphone will not budge. He thinks of Mrs. McCormick's blue tag and worries about a possible explanation. His face is beginning to feel hot and his breath comes in short huffs. The noise has stopped and Bernie thinks maybe he's frightened whatever it was away.

Finally, Bernie tries another flush and the microphone comes bobbing back to the surface of the water. Bernie grabs it, wipes it off, then sits down on the john, his armpits soaked. He plays the tape, hoping for a secret message. All he can hear is the swish of water and his own labored breathing. He considers playing it backwards, but can't figure out how. He puts the tape player back in the drawer.

That night he dreams of spaceships, of kind creatures who make soft music in the darkness between galaxies. They love him, their small human specimen. They even find him a mate, a lovely being, slightly humanoid, from some far off star system. His dreams are chaotic and exciting and when he wakes up, he's sad. He moves slowly, still in the sway of the dreams. He almost forgets how frightening the voices are and wishes he could gather his courage, then head for the shower. But he can't face that cubicle, not yet. He continues sponging off.

After seven weeks of such bathing and double-deodorizing himself, Bernie decides to brave the shower once more. Maybe what he heard was in his mind. His mother always said he had an overactive imagination. By now the voices have surely gone away. He's not heard so much as a single beep in any part of his apartment for over a week.

It occurs to him that before he enters the shower, perhaps he should clean the place in case something happens. He wants it to be perfect. He vacuums, then wipes over the few pieces of wooden furniture. He washes the glass in the sink, dries it and puts it away.

By two-o'clock, Bernie is satisfied that his modest apartment, which might possibly go down in the history books as the first site of alien contact, will do nicely. He smiles, thinking how silly it is for him to expect any kind of encounter. How impossible! Yet, his head is spinning. His hands are now shaking in big movements, like an obsessed maestro. He remembers the feeling he had as a boy of being watched. Someone, somewhere was observing him, and waiting. He recalls how he stood on the hill behind his house one night, stood until his legs went numb. Nothing but the dark heavens and that nagging feeling that he wasn't alone. And now, after all those aching years, whatever it was is coming for him. Instead of being afraid, he feels excited, alive. At last, something to look forward to.

Bernie gathers his best clothes, the black wool suit he bought for his mother's funeral, and the wingtip shoes with the silk socks. He dresses, careful not to crease his shirt while he bends to put on the slacks.

Bernie enjoys tying the slender strings of his shoes. They make him feel elegant somehow, exact. He buffs the leather with his handkerchief though he knows it can't get any shinier. He rubs anyway, taking his time, enjoying the back and forth movement.

He turns on the shower full-blast. He figures he can make more sense of the communication with the water going strong. He puts down the lid of the toilet, not wanting his new friends to be faced with the open mouth of the commode when they first materialize.

He closes the door. The room steams up quickly. Bernie can barely see his reflection in the mirror when he smiles, his face all blurry with condensation. He listens.

There it is, the deep vibration he's heard before. He touches the walls of the shower before he enters. He can sense a pattern, a possible meaning. Satisfied, Bernie steps in and waits.

VISITING JACKIE

What I remember most is the sound of Mother's voice as it filtered through the wooden floor up to my second-story bedroom, dipping and curving about in the air, much like the road that led to our old house on top of Grab-A-Nickel Hill, the asphalt hugging the mountain in that same haphazard way. I couldn't understand any of the words, but I recognized the tunes, hymns mostly—"In the Garden," "The Old Rugged Cross."

Her singing jarred me, tipped me over to the edge of my bed. I hated how her thin trill imitated the women who performed solos at church. Ever since I'd turned twelve, I'd been mad at the world, especially angry at anyone happy enough to warble with no care for anyone else's ears. I couldn't explain the rage, but most of it was directed at Mother and her constant barrage of music. Maybe it had something to do with my little sister, Jackie, being shipped away.

I couldn't tolerate the way Mother's sound lingered in my brain, the echo of her whiny voice following me to school and even out onto the playground. And I especially hated the way she woke me up each day. I'd hear her shift songs on her way up the stairs, going from a hymn to Handle's Messiah, a wispy rendition of "Arise, shine, for thy Light is come." She was pleased with her wit, but after what seemed like a thousand mornings, the joke got old.

Everything was a song with her, at least that's how it seemed to me. I don't remember exactly when the singing started, maybe the year Jackie went away, maybe before. Most of the time, Mother stuck to the familiar hymns. But every once in a while, she'd launch into a Beatles' song—"I Want to Hold Your Hand" and "She Loves You." She'd increase the volume on the 'yeah, yeah, yeah,' parts until it was all I could do to keep from telling her to shut the hell up. I'd only begun to notice some of the other kids using cuss words, and I hadn't said any out loud. But in my mind I thought them and got a little thrill each time I found an appropriate occasion for one.

It seemed forever since she actually spoke to me, except to remind me of my homework or to tell me to do the dishes. I could keep track of her easily by listening for her song and gauge the exact moment before she'd be at my door to check on my progress with math. The system worked well. It allowed me plenty of time to put away my library book and take out pencil and paper, plaster a studious look on my face before she peered in at me.

When I came downstairs for a snack, I could see her bending over the table in the living room with Pledge in one hand, my old underwear in the other, singing, "This is my story/ this is my song/ Praising my Savior/all the day long." Over and over she'd sing, a crazy litany, her weak soprano scraping along, marking each hour of the day.

At first it didn't bother me so much. I figured this love affair with notes and measures would pass like some flu bug. But the singing didn't go away. Rather, it grew and by most evenings, my mother's voice sounded hoarse and ragged. I spent as much time away from home as I could.

Mostly, I explored the woods behind our house. One spring, I discovered all kinds of new growth: the tiny bluets, each blossom smaller than my fingernail, yet perfect, the blue darkening at the edges, a yellow star at the center; and the laurel, heavy white and purple buds hanging on dark waxy leaves, the bushes creating secret places, shadowy habitats for rabbits and ground squirrels. I watched as the mountains slowly turned from brown to new green under the clear April sky.

And I was happy to skip along trails made by the neighborhood kids and watch the sun streak through the trees, splotches of light and dark that fit together tight as puzzle pieces. I liked puzzles. They made sense to me. Sometimes they were the only thing that did and I felt better after putting together a jigsaw alone in my room, like I'd somehow improved the world by taking the jagged parts and linking them to create a beautiful picture.

But Mother's singing disturbed the peace I created for myself, irritating me the way a mosquito bite will itch its way under your skin and go all red and puffy. I still recall how my muscles would tense up each time I heard her. Even now, when I hear a certain melody, I think back about what it was like then, growing up with my mother's voice lifted in song, my little sister torn away from us as surely as if Death itself had grabbed her.

Jackie was only six years old when she went to live in a group home a state away. She was cute with long blond curls and clear blue eyes. I'd waited such a long time for a sister, six whole years, by the time I got Jackie, I was old enough to take care of her the same way I'd rocked and patted my doll babies. She was almost like a doll herself, tiny and delicate, much smaller than I was when I was little. In my baby pictures, I was a kid with sprigs of brown, straight hair poking out in odd directions. I had shiny round cheeks that the kids at school used to call 'chipmunk cheeks.' It was true, they looked stuffed full of something. I hated the way they bulged out, but at least I made mostly A's on my tests. It was my one consolation. I was smart. But I'd rather have had a delicate face and a small, upturned nose like Jackie's.

Of course, she paid a price for her good looks and my brains cost me, too. We both gained something, lost something. I didn't know who was keeping tabs, but balancing things out was important to somebody.

At first, I wasn't sure just how far from normal my sister was. I mean, my friends had siblings who did some pretty bizarre things, like the time Mike Robin's brother jumped from the roof of the house onto the shed and broke his leg. He was pretending to be what he called The Amazing Frog Boy. Of course, no one had ever heard of Frog Boy and we all thought the kid was a little strange. Jackie was worse than that. Each day I noticed something new that stamped Jackie as odd.

She didn't eat the way the other kids her age ate. She wouldn't touch candy or cookies, things most children love. The only thing she really liked was 'peachers' and 'begetables and beeth.' Baby food. At four, she was still eating it straight from the jar. And she talked to herself all the time, asking and answering her own questions in a way that sounded like music. I knew she wasn't like the other kids long before my parents took me into the doctor's office to have him explain it. I knew by the way the other kids left her out and she didn't even mind. She was in her own little world where no one else could enter. Except me. Sometimes I could join her, though not often, but I learned early on to take what I could get.

As if all those clues weren't enough, Jackie gave me another to make sure I knew she was something special. It happened one Saturday afternoon when all the kids were playing in the sunshine on our dead-end street. Whenever Mother sent us outside, my job was to keep an eye on Jackie. She stayed in the yard most of the time, flipping a ball up in the air and talking in a low voice to herself. I anchored myself close by. But sometimes I'd forget about Jackie. I was busy with freeze-tag or cowboys and Indians.

Every kid in the neighborhood knew not to go into Old Man Green's perfectly manicured yard. I'd told Jackie about Old Man Green many times and she usually listened to me and stayed away. This day she forgot.

Green didn't have any children, a rare thing in our neighborhood. And he hated kids. He'd chase any living creature out of his yard with a baseball bat which he kept handy on his front porch. If somebody accidentally threw a ball into his shrubs, it stayed there until it rotted. And the best way to get even with an enemy was to toss his favorite toy into the flower garden. The victim could kiss it goodbye forever.

Imagine how I felt when I was playing four-square in the road with a bunch of my friends when suddenly I saw Jackie charging into the forbidden zone with the zeal of a bull elephant. I ran from my hard-earned spot in the server's square to grab her before she went too far.

But I was clumsy and slow, and before I knew it, she'd plodded right into Old Man Green's tulips, trampling the heavy buds as she went. By the time I'd reached her, Old Man Green had his bat in hand, and his red face huffed swear words at us both.

"If she's too goddam dumb to stay out of my yard, then you'd better keep her out. You hear?" His spittle fell on my upturned face. No grown-up had cussed at me before.

"Let's get out of here, Jackie. He's mean," I said in the strongest voice I could muster. I didn't care if he chased me with his bat. He'd called Jackie dumb. I'd never let anyone call her that. And he acted like there was something wrong with me, too. He lumped us together and I didn't like it. I knew I wasn't like her, but I wondered if something in me might get crazy, some hidden thing that might pop out as suddenly as chicken pox. When he raised his bat to threaten us, anger propelled me out of his yard faster than I thought

Anne Clinard Barnhill

I could go. And I dragged Jackie behind me by her skinny arm.

"Don't ever go in there again. He's a bad man. A BAD MAN. Understand?" I shook her shoulder just a little for emphasis. She wouldn't look at me, but that wasn't unusual. I could tell she'd already gone somewhere else, her eyes fixed far away. She gritted her teeth, a habit she'd had since the first tiny row of seedpearls appeared on her gums. "Stop gritting." Already she'd worn them down so that they were angled funny. I was trying to break her of it.

Each afternoon when I came home from school, I'd find Mother and Jackie working at the kitchen table. Mother was trying to teach Jackie how to count to ten, her ABC's and her colors. I'd throw my books on the counter, grab a cold glass of milk, eat a couple of cookies and do my homework right then to get it out of the way. Sometimes I thought I'd go nuts if I heard the alphabet song one more time, but Jackie was getting it and she'd learned to sing it all the way through. Now Mother was helping her learn what the letters looked like. Jackie tried hard and sometimes it I could almost forget the strange stuff she did. I'd look at her little cute face, the blond curls, the sweet smile and I'd almost have myself believing she'd be all right.

Jackie might have looked like a little angel, but she didn't always act like one. Sometimes living with her wasn't easy. One day after school I raced home to catch Bonanza on TV. It was the episode where Hoss finds the Leprechauns and I couldn't wait. I took the stairs two at a time so I could change into my play clothes and plop in front of the old black and white set in my mother's bedroom. When I opened the door to my room, I couldn't believe what I saw. Scattered over my floor were doll parts-arms, legs, heads, torsos-and standing in the middle of the mess was Jackie, sort of jumping in place. She held the head of my bride doll by its golden hair and was flipping her fingers against the plastic face. Bridey's eyes blinked open, then snapped shut with each new attack.

"MOM! I'm going to KILL Jackie!!" My voice tore from my throat and I stepped quickly over the mutilated toys to save my Bridey, or what was left of her. I screamed again at Jackie, but she didn't do anything. All she did was stand there and look at me like there was nothing strange in that room, nothing malicious in her act of destruction.

"What's the matter?" Mother stood at the doorway, her hands covered in flour. Then she took a look around. "Oh my God." Mother's face turned white and for a minute she didn't say a word. Her eyes reminded me of caged birds, wild and looking for a way out. Then she put her arms around me and whispered.

"She didn't mean to … …she doesn't know any better." She stooped over to retrieve Bridey's legs which were protruding from her wedding dress. "I'll get your daddy to fix this." Mother patted my back for a long time. Finally, she turned to me, her hand still on my shoulder and said, "Don't be mad at her." She left the two of us there and I heard her humming softly as she went back to the kitchen. "Stay with Jackie. Don't leave her by herself," she called to me from downstairs.

I stared at Jackie, the fury still in me. She looked down at her hands and started giggling. It was a zany kind of laugh, full of the devil, as my grandmother would have said. And then she started talking to herself in that strange melodic way she had. She never referred to herself in the first person, but kept a safe third-person distance.

"Is her sister mad at her? Does her sister want to kill her? Her sister's angry…Why is her sister angry?" Over and over under her breath until I felt my heart soften, go to a sort of mush.

"It's okay, Jackie. I'm not mad. I'm not." I pulled her to me and she stood stiff while I hugged her.

Soon after the doll incident, my parents sent Jackie away. They told me there were special doctors in Pittsburgh who knew just what to do with kids like Jackie. They told me the doctors could help Jackie become more normal. I wanted that more than anything, so I tried not to cry that first time when my parents and Jackie headed for Pennsylvania. I couldn't go along because school was still in session. I didn't mind missing the trip because I didn't want to tell Jackie good-bye. Besides, I really liked Mrs. Talley, my baby-sitter.

The following Tuesday, I didn't hurry home after school, even though I knew Mother would be back. Instead, I followed the path through the woods, then struck my own trail and discovered a meadow at the top of the hill. I stood at the edge and lost myself in the sweet sunshine. I stood for a long time, the light washing over me. I thought about Jackie and why she was the way she was. I wondered why God did stuff to little kids. I tried to lay blame, but there wasn't any place to put it.

Exhausted, I hiked home, my clothes hot and growing sticky with sweat. Finally, I headed for my own yard, my own room. I heard Mother as I reached the mailbox at the end of the driveway.

"Oh, Soul, are you weary and troubled?/ No light in the darkness you see/ Turn your eyes upon Jesus," Her voice was rough, gravelly and it sounded as if she'd been singing forever. She was cooking pot roast, peeling potatoes and cutting onions. I watched from the kitchen door as she wiped her wet cheek with the back of her arm, her knife in one hand, the onion in the other.

That night at supper, I was afraid to mention Jackie, terrified of what might happen if her name was spoken. My parents acted cheerful, but I noticed they didn't eat much, and they, too, said nothing of their trip to Pittsburgh.

I wanted Jackie to get well, to be like all the other little kids. I kept that picture of her in my mind, of us growing up together, me giving her advice about boys, discussing our

What You Long For

weird parents, laughing and giggling in our room after we'd been told to settle down and go to sleep. Part of me knew it was impossible, but another part believed in miracles.

I took to praying. I don't mean just occasional prayer spoken off the top of your head. I mean 'deliberate petition.' I learned about tenacity in Sunday School when the teacher told us about the widow who kept bugging a certain judge for justice until he finally gave in, just so she'd shut up. That's the kind of praying I did for Jackie. I wanted justice for her and there wasn't anything fair about her being sent away and her being 'different.'

I begged God until my throat hurt and my eyes made wet spots on my pillow. My ears clogged and my hair was damp from the tears and still I prayed. I imagined my prayers rising up to heaven, a silver stream of words washing over the ears of all the angels, trickling into the very ear of God Himself. My prayers would sound like the sweetest music and His Ear would lap them up.

I didn't let up because Jackie's life depended on it. I had to plead hard and most nights I prayed myself to sleep.

I remembered the story about the woman who touched the hem of Jesus' garment. She didn't really bother the Lord. Instead, she almost stole her healing away from him. That's what I wanted Jackie to do: steal up to Jesus and swipe at his robe. If she could just touch it, she'd be healed.

So far, though I was faithful in beseeching the Lord on her behalf, nothing had changed. Jackie still flipped her doll heads, she still ground her teeth and chattered to herself in that sing-song way. But maybe the special school would be the answer, just like Dad said. Maybe she could reach out and grab Jesus' garment in Pittsburgh.

Later that summer, Dad, Mother and I packed up the camper to visit Jackie. I didn't know what to expect. We were going for Jackie's birthday. She was turning six and she'd been at the group home for almost four months.

We'd only talked about Jackie once since she'd been gone. My dad explained that no matter how hard it was to leave Jackie, no matter how much we missed her, we had to give the group home a try. He said when you really love someone, you do what's best for that person, not what feels best for yourself.

I kept wondering what it would be like to leave home, to be without your family. I couldn't imagine. The thought of going away scared me, and I couldn't stand the idea of being away from my parents. I thought I'd even miss Mother's singing. Well, maybe. I didn't dare try to put myself in Jackie's shoes.

Though I wouldn't let myself think about how she must feel, sometimes quick-crazy images flashed through my mind. Jackie sitting alone in her room. Or crying into her pillow. Or being punished without me there to comfort her. I worried about her gritting her teeth more than ever.

On that first trip, Mother woke me early. As usual, she sang, but on this special day, she veered from her routine and wandered into new territory—Negro spirituals.

"Are you ready for the kingdom? Oh yeah." She stuck her round face into my room, her mouth pretty with bright lipstick. She snapped her fingers in rhythm to the gospel song.

"I'm getting up. Give me time." My anger seeped out everywhere and my voice clenched up its fist. That year, I had a hard time controlling it. "Do you have to sing?" I mumbled this last part, afraid I'd hurt her feelings by mentioning the weird habit. Usually, I didn't mind causing Mother pain, but I didn't want to spoil the weekend. I wanted everything to be perfect for Jackie.

I hurried once Mother had left me to myself and slipped on the outfit I'd chosen. The red skirt was new and I wore a matching striped blouse. At the store Mother insisted that the skirt skim the tops of my knees, which was way longer than the other girls wore theirs. But though the skirt was longer than I liked, I wore it anyway because red was Jackie's favorite color. And besides, Jackie didn't care whether my skirt was the fashionable length or not. All she cared about was seeing me, seeing the whole family.

I was looking forward to spending the night in our pop-up camper. Jackie would take the top bunk and I'd sleep below her. Each night I'd tell her stories. My words would weave us together and we'd laugh at the cockeyed tales. Jackie liked scary ones and funny ones, so with each story I tried to outdo myself. I thought all week about what I'd say. For sure, the spooky "Who's Got My Talie Toe" and maybe one about dental hygiene. Jackie considered teeth funny and loved to hear about visits to the dentist.

When we were together, Jackie would call me 'Jet,' her pet name for me. She explained that she thought my face was shaped like a jet airplane, but I didn't see it. Jets were angular and sleek and my face didn't fit such a description. But I was happy she saw me that way, and I looked forward to hearing her sing her original composition, "Jet-Shaped Face." She made it up all by herself with what she called her 'musical ears.'

While we packed the car, my parents acted like we were going to an amusement park or some such thing. Of course, we *were* planning to go to Kennywood Park where there was a huge rollercoaster. Jackie loved those rides, though you'd have thought she'd have been afraid of them. She used to smile each time the train would climb up to the sky, then hurl us toward the earth. She'd scream and scream and the minute we hopped off, she wanted to get on again. I couldn't wait to try the one at Kennywood.

Dad told me there was a zoo, also. When we went to the dinky French Creek Animal Farm in West Virginia, Jackie liked the petting zoo in particular, where she could actually touch the animals. The last time we went, she followed a billy goat around for ever, pulling its tail down to cover its butt.

She liked a sense of order, everything in its place. I knew the Pittsburgh zoo would be a lot better and I wondered what Jackie would do when she saw exotic animals like elephants and lions.

But though we were planning to do fun things, I knew the activities were mostly for Jackie. And I didn't understand why my folks forced such a festive mood during the journey. For me, the trip meant a knot in my stomach and tears threatening at the back of my throat. And the dread of saying good-bye to Jackie once more.

She was waiting at the door when we got there, her hair cut short and blunt, the curls gone. Her face was red and roughened by the sun, her shirttail out on one side and the plaid skirt she wore hiked up in the back. She'd never liked skirts, but I guess she, too, wanted to dress up. Or maybe they made her.

A fat woman dressed in a white uniform stood guard beside her, one large black hand on Jackie's small shoulder. Jackie started toward us the minute she saw us walking in from the parking lot, but I saw that hand restrain her. When we reached the door, the woman could no longer hold her and she rushed to us, threw her arms around Mother. Mother held her, the longest hug I'd ever seen her give. Then Jackie embraced Dad, and, finally, me.

The nurse led us to Jackie's room, one she shared with another girl. Her weekend bag was packed. Gunbaby, her favorite doll, poked out from the top of the zipper. Gunbaby was the only doll that hadn't had his head ripped off. He was all of a piece and looked something like Daniel Boone with breeches and a rifle molded along with his regular body parts. No way could Jackie pull that head off.

Other kids gathered at Jackie's doorway. They watched, their eyes wild and strange, as we picked up the suitcase and started to leave.

"Where going? Where?" said one little boy with bright orange hair. I watched, stared, even though I knew it wasn't polite, as his head jerked to one side over and over. The big girl behind him sucked her thumb and drool oozed down her chin.

"Home? Go home?" Yet another face intruded, a black girl about thirteen. My age. Her hair was matted into short pigtails and she wore a striped shirt with plaid slacks. I cringed at the combination.

Suddenly, I wanted out of there. The air was too hot, too thick with people. Jackie seemed to disappear, blend into this strange collection. It was hard to tell her from the others. I didn't want her to be a part of this gang of weirdoes. I wanted her to be with us, Mother, Dad and me. I pushed through the little cluster and Jackie followed me.

She ignored them all. She didn't even notice when the boy with the nodding head grabbed my hand. She hurried for the front door full speed ahead. My hand was gooey from where the redhead held onto me, gripping me tight until the nurse made him let go. I brushed my sticky fingers against the new skirt and ran with Jackie to the car.

That night for supper we ate at the Golden Arches. Mother worried about what Jackie might find to eat there and we were all surprised when she said she wanted fries and a milkshake.

"I didn't know you liked french fries, honey. That's great. I'm glad you're trying new things." Mother smiled and Dad tussled Jackie's hair with his big palm. She and I dipped our fries in ketchup and slurped our chocolate shakes. I watched as hope bloomed across Mother's features while Jackie gobbled up real food. I, too, thought maybe my prayers were being answered.

"What do you do at the group home, Jackie?" I wanted to know if she was getting better or if it was just my imagination.

"Her sister wants to know what she does. Her sister asked her a question. Ballet? Does she take ballet?" Jackie answered me like usual, more with a question than an answer, but I knew what she meant.

"That's great. Ballet, huh. Can you show me a dance?" I didn't mean for her to demonstrate in the restaurant. That she might hadn't even occurred to me. But before we could stop her, she was pirouetting around the place and every eye was on her. She didn't care. On and on she spun, all over the restaurant, bumping into people, spilling drinks, until Dad caught her by the elbow and pulled her back to our table.

Mother shushed her and Jackie began to cry. The fries I'd eaten sank like cement in my stomach.

The weekend passed quickly and soon the time came to say our good-byes. I would learn that the time always came.

Dad swung into the lot in front of Jackie's building and parked in the visitor slot. Seeing that word, 'Visitor,' printed in white on the curb made me feel funny, like we weren't a real family. My lunch sloshed around in my stomach. Jackie begged for another story as Dad turned off the engine.

"We don't have time, honey. Gotta get on the road. Gotta get home before dark." His thin brown hair fell across his face when he turned to talk to us in the back seat. He pushed it away with his hand and I noticed his skin was grayish, the color of dustballs under my bed. Mother was quiet.

"Just one more. Please. I can make it short." I pleaded, my voice whiny.

"No. Not this time." He answered in his no-nonsense voice and I realized I'd lost. I grabbed Jackie's hand as she pulled on the door handle. We scooted out together.

We walked behind Mother and Dad. Both of us dawdled, dragging our feet, stopping to smell the flowers that lined the sidewalk. I didn't want to leave her, not here, not with all those loonies. She didn't belong. Why didn't anyone see that but me? She was smarter than those other kids and so much prettier. She didn't drool.

My stomach tightened.

Jackie led us to her room where Mother put her clean, folded clothes away in the dresser drawer. While she worked, she and Jackie sang silly songs. This time Mother's singing didn't bother me. I even joined in and did the motions with Jackie for "I'm a little teapot." Jackie showed us some of her drawings, told us about her ballet lessons and demonstrated the positions. Mother finally finished with the clothes, snapped the lid of the empty suitcase shut and shoved it under Jackie's bed. Mother's cheeks looked sunken and even her red lipstick didn't do much to brighten her face. She spoke in a whisper.

"That about does it," she said soft as a lullaby.

Dad wrapped Jackie in his arms, made a shell of himself around her. "Give me a big hug." Jackie held on long and tight. She'd never been one for hugs and kisses, but she'd learned to allow them, even the really extended touches. Now she made a show of her kisses, stretching her arms open and smacking her lips with a loud, wet noise.

After Dad was finished, Mother cupped Jackie's small cheeks in her hands. They gazed at each other.

"When can Jackie come home, Mommy? Jackie wants to come home." Jackie's eyes teared up and Mother stood speechless. Dad reached to take Jackie into his lap. He didn't look at Mother, who seemed unable to move.

"They're trying to help you, Jackie. Help you learn. You work hard and you'll be home soon. I promise." His voice broke just a little. Mother turned her back to us.

Finally, it was my turn to say good-bye. I held Jackie, my eyes squeezed together hard.

"Bye, Jet," she yelled in my ear. I felt Dad's hand on my shoulder, the signal to let her go.

By the time I'd curled myself into a ball in the back seat of the car, my head pounded. Dad backed out of the parking space and I unrolled myself to wave to Jackie one last time. She stood inside the storm door of the building, the same fat nurse beside her, that hand again on her shoulder. Dad began to drive away very slowly.

Suddenly, Jackie broke loose from the nurse, opened the door and ran after the car. She was all arms and legs flailing in the air. I stared, unable to believe she was following us, unable to tear my eyes from her small body framed by the rear window.

"Dad! Stop the car! She's running after us. Stop!" I heard him suck in his breath, then he looked into the rearview mirror. His throat made a loud sound as he swallowed. Mother hunched her shoulders just a little. She stared ahead.

Dad didn't respond. He kept driving the same slow pace as when he started. I watched as the nurse lumbered after Jackie, caught her and bound her in those large, black arms. We drove on.

No one spoke. We didn't utter a word for the whole trip home. We were wrapped in silence, eggshell-thin. A sound would have broken us.

A TELEPHONE MINISTRY

"YOU ARE A DIRTY BASTARD!" Velma Adams hissed into the telephone, her voice angry as the whisper of Satan himself. She enunciated each syllable to be certain her priest, Father Bottom, understood. Then she slammed the receiver down fast. Velma wiped her fingerprints from the telephone like the criminals did on the Perry Mason reruns she watched every day. After the black receiver was buffed to a glossy shine, Velma realized she needn't have bothered. Her own prints on her own phone would be perfectly logical. Oh well.

She considered her vocabulary and decided that she should have said simply, "You bastard!" but curse words didn't form easily on her lips. This was her first try. She'd get better.

Never in her sixty-seven years had Velma vented anger. Not when her younger sister, Vera, cut Velma's best party dress to ribbons in an attempt to weave a pot holder. Not when her husband, Lloyd, kissed a stranger smack on the lips welcoming the New Year back in 1969.

But she'd done it now. She'd loosened the lid on her own pressure cooker and released a steam of rage that had been boiling up for years. Humph. That new priest, Father Charles he wanted to be called. So like the modern church to forego formalities and put the priest on a first-name basis with everyone, including that snooty Martha Long. Velma couldn't stand the thought of being on familiar terms with such a man. He deserved what he got. Yes, he deserved it all right. Velma smiled to herself, though her hands still shook.

She walked to the refrigerator and poured herself a tall glass of diet Coke over ice. Mmmm. Cool. That's what she was now, cool, like the guy in the *DIE HARD* movies. He certainly was no stranger to dirty language. Velma decided her vocabulary could use a bit of spice for her new purpose and *DIE HARD* was about as peppery as she could imagine. Not that she'd have considered viewing such a film on her own. No, her thirteen-year-old grandson talked her into renting the video. If she'd known what a foul-mouthed person *DIE HARD* was, she wouldn't have consented. But John had begged and pleaded until she and Lloyd caved in, a mistake, no doubt, but at least she'd enjoyed the movie. It caused her to consider what life must be like for those who take things into their own hands.

Like vengeance. It is Mine, saith the Lord. She knew that. But just this once, she wanted a little for herself. It felt so right to dial his number, imagine him racing to the phone. Perhaps he thought the call would announce a death in the church or a couple in crisis. Or maybe he harbored a secret dream in his heart, a dream of Martha Long donating her estate to the church. Velma tried to picture his face as he heard a low voice curse him for the dog he was. She could see that scraggly moustache twitch as he slammed down the receiver. Let him get angry. Let him reap what he'd sown.

Velma remembered the first Sunday Fr. Bottom preached in St. Pious Episcopal's new chapel. He strolled down the aisle in his cassock and Velma could hear the swish, swish of him as he passed her pew. His eyes glared straight ahead and he didn't even nod at Velma the way Father Peterson used to. Instead, he tilted his head slightly toward Martha Long where she perched up front on her family pew.

Dear, dear Father Peterson. Now there was a priest who knew how to relate to his parishioners. He'd come for Sunday dinner and rave about Velma's chicken casserole. And the way he carried on about her beef stew and homemade rolls, why, it made her blush fresh as a school girl.

She'd invited Fr. Bottom for lunch, tempting him with baked ham. It was at that point that he told her he was a vegetarian, of all things. She should have realized something was wrong with him because he had those weak, watery eyes. She'd thought it was allergies, but now she knew the real reason. As far as Velma was concerned, you couldn't trust a man who didn't enjoy a thick, juicy steak.

Not only did he avoid meat, he refused anything containing animal products. No milk or eggs, not even lard. Velma couldn't imagine what was left to sustain him, but he'd explained that Vegans, that's what he called himself, were eating according to God's plan. When he said the word 'Vegan', she'd immediately thought of the strange man on television, the one with the pointed ears on that old show, Star Trek. But when she tried to converse with Fr. Bottom about aliens, he'd explained that those were VULCANS, not Vegans.

Velma didn't like the look of him, no matter what name he went by. Fortyish, with bushy hair worn long, the gray strands well over his collar, Fr. Bottom sported a wild-looking beard. He wore a tweed jacket on every occasion and Velma thought it looked ridiculous with his clerical collar. His skin was pale and those puny-looking eyes gave her the creeps.

Velma especially didn't approve of the way the Father pretended not to see you unless you were right up on him, like the time she'd been walking to the grocery store and he passed her going the opposite direction. She said good morning, but he didn't bat an eye, just tried to look buried in thought, like his righteous ruminations were more important than a hello to Velma.

When she'd introduced herself on the very first Sunday he gave the sacraments, he'd barely acknowledged her. Though she'd explained that she'd been a member of St. Pious her entire life, had taught Sunday School for thirty years and was in charge of the Altar Guild, Dr. Bottom just smiled briefly, barely meeting her stare. He made her feel like she wasn't really there, like she didn't matter one way or the other.

But that was two long years past. She'd tried, oh really tried to accept Dr. Bottom. When he called God 'She' sometimes, Velma sucked in deep breaths, held them one, two, three. In her mind, she attempted to picture God as female, Her arms wrapped around Velma, long gray hair twisting like cat's tails. But somehow, the vision always turned into the usual God with flowing robes and big muscled arms—the Michelangelo version. And she felt so much more comfortable in those strong arms.

Velma heard something stir.

"What are you doing up at this hour?" Lloyd squinted into the kitchen's dim light, a bluish-green glow from the microwave and the oven clock. Velma chose the phone in the kitchen for this well-lit reason.

"Nothing, dear. I had a bit of an upset stomach. Thought a little Coke might help. Go back to bed." She forced her voice to its usual smoothness, though inside she trembled.

"You'll think I'm crazy, but I thought I heard you talking to somebody." Lloyd stood in his red polka-dot boxers and white tee shirt. How Velma loathed his use of underwear as pajamas. She'd rather he wore anything other than that getup. She'd prefer nothing at all. That unexpected thought shocked her and she suddenly recalled how Lloyd used to look when he was bending over her making love, the hunch of his shoulders and the feel of his mouth on her neck. She hadn't considered Lloyd like that in years. Maybe the *DIE*

HARD movie had affected her more than she realized. Perhaps it had touched off an entire series of changes in her body chemistry. She felt herself go all loose, like her bones were coming unhinged. She knew she needed to get a grip.

"You must be hearing things, dear." She waved Lloyd back to their bedroom with her free hand. "I'll be along in a minute."

After he'd waddled off, his shorts swaying like a railroad warning light, Velma sank down onto the chair at her end of the table. Suddenly, her entire body shook.

"Dear Lord, what am I doing? Help me. Oh, help me." Velma's whisper echoed in the emptiness. She thought of Dr. Bottom, his phone ringing, shattering his sleep the way he'd blasted hers for nights on end, forcing her to think about nothing but him and his rude ways. She considered again his confused "Hello? Hello? Who is this?" on the line.

She smiled. Let him suffer. Let him answer his line forever in a blaring telephone hell.

She lifted the receiver and dialed his number again. One for the road. She'd memorized the digits in case she found a phone when she was out and about. That way, she could call him at will, whenever the urge struck.

"Hello? Hello? Who IS this?" He sounded angry, very angry.

"You... You... weirdo!" Velma whispered low, disguising her voice as best she could. She heard a click. He'd hung up. She immediately dialed again. Busy signal.

Well, that was enough for the first night. Tomorrow would be a bright, new day.

Velma splashed cologne on her chest, right above her bra in the crease between her breasts. Then she added a touch to her underarms, a dab behind each ear and on her wrists. Today the Altar Guild luncheon would be held at Martha Long's home. That snooty-toot loved gossip more than Bible verses and always hoped to get some during the session. During their prayer time, Martha practically salivated when some innocent woman would make a special request for her marriage or one of her grandchildren. Martha always coaxed out the juicy details. She said it was so the group could pray specifically to the Lord, but Velma knew better.

Velma smiled. Her lips were sealed, as always.

"I'll be back in a couple of hours, Lloyd. Take out some ground turkey to thaw and we'll stir fry tonight." Velma enjoyed having Lloyd work at home as he'd done for the last year since he'd taken early retirement. He was happy to run a few errands for her and the money he earned as a consultant was even better than he'd made at the textile company where he'd put in thirty-five years.

"Okay, hon. Move mountains." Lloyd didn't have much use for church and rarely attended. Velma might persuade him to visit at Christmas but he always sat in the very back pew. He couldn't understand her grievances about Fr. Bottom, though he frequently made fun of the name. Velma enjoyed his jokes but she resented the way he dismissed her complaints. He hadn't heard the flimsy excuses the Father had made to avoid having dinner with Velma. And Lloyd had the irritating philosophy of live and let live. When she'd told him about the Father's strange eating habits, Lloyd'd simply said "Good. All the more for me."

As she drove to Martha's house, Velma considered the Father once again. Oh, she might have been able to overlook those ghastly sermons about the importance of using recycled toilet paper or promoting social justice by giving up red meat. And she could have ignored the little slights he'd aimed her way, his looking past her each time they ran into each other. She could have prayed away her anger, the way she'd prayed herself into forgiveness her whole life. But finally, he went too far. Finally, it came down to the Spring Rummage Sale, Martha Long's soy-based quiche, and Velma's cold-oven pound cake.

The first day of the sale had been a sunny Saturday in April. Already, the tulips were pushing their way into the air, the daffodils in full bloom.

She'd been so inspired by the warm weather that she'd baked more cakes for the sale than usual. An even dozen of the most perfect pound cakes you've ever seen. Of course, Velma would never have said that out loud. She didn't have to. Her cakes were famous in Lincolnton, North Carolina and the entire congregation told her over and over how delicious they were. People raved about their light texture, how moist each piece was. And the flavor, a slight touch of lemon with a melt-in-your-mouth goodness that was hard to deny. Velma loved the cakes as much as anyone, especially the rich top crust, a combination of soft and crunchy, the best part. She took pride in those cakes, though she knew it was a sin. But her mother'd told her a thousand times that cooking was the only thing Velma knew how to do and Velma didn't think it was fair to force humility about one's singular gift. She allowed herself that one little thing—satisfaction in the kitchen.

"Look at all those fattening cakes!" Martha Long had declared when she saw Velma and Lloyd carrying in a box-load each. "Of course, I made quiche and dear Velma, as luck would have it, I found a recipe that used soy so dear Father Bottom can enjoy it, too. He's already bought four slices."

Velma sliced her cakes.

Though some cakes had been sold whole in advance, bringing a full twelve dollars each, the Rummage Sale workers discovered long ago that they'd make more money selling them by the slice. And, as the sale continued, the slices would become thinner and thinner.

Velma kept busy behind her booth, cutting and scraping crumbs from her knife. Suddenly, Fr. Bottom stood before her.

"I understand I can buy a piece of cake?" He averted his eyes.

"Tell you what. Since this is your first year, I'll just give you a slice. You can pay for seconds." Velma was so proud of herself. She'd practiced Christian charity and heaped coals upon the good Father's head.

"Thanks. I don't usually eat sweets, but several folks told me I ought to try your cake. So, I figured why not? Seems to be the thing to do." He picked at a crumb from his paper plate.

"Well, I know it's filled with eggs and milk, but maybe this one time won't hurt you." Velma felt a victory in the making. She'd convert him yet.

She pretended to go about her business, but she kept her eye on Fr. Bottom. She wanted to see the actual moment when his eyes would glaze over and that familiar look of contentment would settle on his face. The look was the same each time someone sampled her cake and she'd grown fond of watching for it. She could barely wait for him to gobble the remainder of the cake and come back for more.

But the special look didn't come. She kept glancing at him as he chatted with various church members. Not once did his face register ecstasy, or even a ripple of pleasure. He didn't return for seconds. And not one word was said, ever, about her great-grandmother's secret recipe pound cake. That, she could never forgive.

Velma steered her Volkswagen Cabriolet into Martha's driveway and parked next to the garage door, leaving room for several cars beside her. The convertible was her one treat, indulged in after everything else was paid for, including her house. She loved to take the top down and turn up the stereo with Bach blaring full blast. And the car was small so that she could park it with ease. A light tap on the side screen, a quick "Come on in" and Velma was once again inside Martha Long's opulent home. A part of Velma enjoyed the luxury of heirloom furniture and silk wallpaper while another side couldn't help tallying up how much it must have cost.

"We're waiting for Dottie Poston. Would you like some iced tea?" Martha was the perfect hostess. Velma noted the tiny heart-shaped sandwiches on a nearby table, fine china and linen napkins lined up in rows, then a bowl of fresh fruit and a plate of fancy-looking cookies, store-bought, as usual. Velma never served anything she hadn't made herself and she considered it a character flaw in those who favored convenience over quality.

"No thanks. Everything looks lovely." Velma always gave a compliment to the hostess, even when it was Martha's turn. Martha looked a little tense as she guided Velma to a seat on the antique velvet couch. Velma could tell that Martha was dying to tell the group something, but for some reason was putting it off. Finally, after allowing a few minutes for chatting, Martha rang her small lunch bell and the room grew quiet.

"Girls, I've got the most dreadful news. I was going to wait for Dottie, but… " She paused for effect. Velma had seen Martha's flair for drama before.

"Oh, go ahead, Martha. It'll serve Dottie right to miss out on something." Mary Beth Hollins still harbored ill-will toward Dottie for the Christmas punch incident. It was Mary Beth's turn as hostess and Dottie had been typically late. By the time she arrived, the sherbet Christmas tree Mary Beth had carved for the punch was in a shapeless blob. She'd never quite forgiven Dottie.

"If you insist." Again, that pause.

Then, in a loud whisper, "You won't believe this. Somebody has been making obscene phone calls to our very own Father Charles." She waited for the surprised intake of breath. Then she continued, "He told me all about it. In strictest confidence, of course. He asked for our prayers." Martha delivered her news with a smug look. Velma watched as incredulous looks appeared on each woman's face. Mary Beth's mouth opened in a dainty red circle, but she didn't issue any sound. Jojo Ingle's hand flew to her full cheeks as she denied the truth of Martha's news. Velma didn't have to fake surprise. She had no idea Fr. Bottom would have the nerve to approach the Alter Guild. She should have known he'd try to enlist the help of the faithful to eradicate the lone dissenter, his nemesis. She suppressed a smile. Imagine, she, Velma Adams, someone's downfall.

"I think we should pray for him right this minute." Mary Beth's lips finally moved from their perfect 'oh'. Prayer was her specialty. She'd bow her head at the first sign of trouble. Used to be she'd petition the Lord while she was driving, but not so often since her accident.

Each head bent at the neck. Except Velma's. Velma kept her eyes focused on the crowns exposed to her. She noticed a couple were wearing thin and Mary Beth's roots were about an inch longer than usual.

"Dear Lord, Please be with our beloved preacher as he battles with the telephone devil. Oh Heavenly Father, give him strength to fight the obscene caller. Amen." Murmured amens rang around the living room.

Velma couldn't stand it. She didn't pray one word, didn't 'amen' and didn't intend to give up her attack just yet. If anything, the prayer made her more determined than ever to expose Fr. Bottom for the charlatan she knew him to be.

"Excuse me." She felt the urge, though not the usual one that plagued older women. The thought almost made her laugh out loud.

Martha whispered to her as she left the group, "Past my bedroom on the left," directions to the bathroom.

Velma could hear the chatter of the women as she walked down the long hall. She passed Martha's bedroom, then doubled back. Inside the large boudoir, she picked up the pink princess telephone on Martha's night stand. She

What You Long For

studied the numbers printed inside the receiver, Martha's phone number. She committed it to memory, just in case she might need it some day. Velma closed the bedroom door.

Slowly and quietly she pressed the buttons, the familiar melody of Fr. Bottom's number soothing her nerves. She heard him pick up.

"Hello. Hello."

Velma whispered the f-word for the first time in her life. Then she growled it once more for good measure.

"I don't know who you are, but you need help." The Father didn't sound the least bit forgiving.

A loud click resounded in her ear. Velma could feel a flush spreading across her chest and cheeks. She was getting to him, that much she could tell. But what if someone found out? What if they discovered who was harassing the minister? Velma didn't want to consider possibilities.

"Velma? Are you all right?" Martha's cajoling voice wheedled its way around the corner.

"Fine. Be right with you." Velma tried to throw her voice, but she wasn't sure it went in the right direction. But Martha's footsteps retreated back to the living room and Velma's secret remained safe for the time being. She quickly said a prayer of thanks and petitioned the Lord for a way to reveal Father Charles for what he truly was—a snobby little man whose personal habits were questionable at best.

Then, almost the moment she'd finished her prayer, she had an idea—what she later knew was Divine Inspiration.

When she rejoined the group, she expected further gossip about the mysterious caller. Instead, an uneasy silence had gathered like pennies in the collection plate. No doubt the women were considering possible action. Velma knew that now was the time to strike, to put her plan into play.

"What have I missed, girls?" Velma smiled, but inside she trembled.

"Not much. We're just wondering what we can do to help poor Father Charles." Martha paused. Velma knew she'd have to draw Martha into her plan the way you had to pull a thick chocolate shake through a straw.

"Well..." Velma no longer shook.

Martha stared at Velma and Velma lowered her eyes. It was a knowing look, just the kind to lure the mettlesome Martha.

"Velma, you know something. What is it?" The room was silent. Velma knew how to whip up a soufflé of interest as well, if not better, than Martha could. She paused.

"I really shouldn't..." Velma again lowered her eyes and crossed her arms. She knew that Martha would wheedle out the news or die trying. Velma could wait, just the way she'd waited on her cakes to bake over the years.

"Now, Velma, if you know something about this, you owe it to us, your sisters in Christ, to tell." Martha's eye shadow was smearing and her face looked moist.

"That's right, Velma. You can't carry the burden alone." Mary Beth was already assuming the prayer position. All faces turned to Velma.

She lifted her head and turned her eyes to the ceiling as if asking permission to spill her news. A peaceful shudder of breath and she began.

"I hate to be the bearer of bad news, but, well, I've heard a little something about our new priest."

All the women leaned forward in their chairs. Velma paused again and let the silence build.

"It seems our own Father Bottom was relieved of duty from his last church under rather mysterious circumstances." Again, Velma rested and took a deep breath as if this news disturbed her so she could hardly continue. The women seemed to hang in the air, their faces suspended, a circle of anticipation.

"Go on, go on, for goodness' sake," said Martha.

"Well, it seems that he had some sort of doings with a woman from California—some animal rights fanatic. It was the talk of his parish or so I've been told." Velma whispered the news and watched as the women broke into loud conversations, their voices buzzing. She sat, silently congratulating herself for concocting such a rich dish. Now the news of his indiscretion would spread over the church like icing, thick and sweet and sinfully delicious.

No one would suspect Velma of any wrong-doing. Instead, when the good Father complained about the phone calls, he would be subjected to a few "um-hums," maybe even a yawn. After all, how seriously could you take a man with a finicky appetite and an unnatural love for animals? Yes, the flavor of scandal was permeating Father Bottom's good name even as sat in his office composing his sermon. Velma was certain that the more he discussed the nasty phone calls, the more disenchanted his parishioners would become. Just a sprinkle of gossip and his time at St. Pious would be cut short.

Then perhaps the church would get a real priest, one who kept the honor of his position, one who enjoyed lunching with his parishioners. One who knew a great piece of cake when he ate one.

KINGS AND DAMSELS

I met Freddy the summer I turned thirteen. That year, the mountains made black shadows against a faultless blue sky; birds signaled in secret code; and dandelion tea, bitter on the tongue, promised superhuman strength. Freddy and his mama were part of the mystery, the red of his mama's hair a sure sign of something.

I was new to the mountains, coming from the steady flatlands of Texas to the wild tangle of West Virginia laurel. My family had packed our stuff into a moving van, twisted our way to a house five miles from town, and settled in. I missed the perfect rectangular blocks with sidewalks made for bike riding, or playing "Snake in the Gully." Here, land hid itself, took strange turns. Waves of earth rolled so that if you followed a trail into the woods, you might end up completely out of sight from home.

That's how I found Freddy. We were unloading the truck and after I'd broken Mom's favorite lamp, she told me to explore my new neighborhood, but she cautioned me against going too far. I don't know why she called it a neighborhood. There were only three other houses on the whole street and lots of woods.

I headed across the front yard, a small, flat area in the V of the valley where our house sat, and took a trail that led straight to the peak that hid our place from the main road. Soon, I'd crested the hill and had seen a chipmunk and a big furry thing I took to be a groundhog. The woods were dark with no human noises except the sound of my tennis shoes scuffing up rocks and leaves. I could smell the fresh, rich odor of earth. I stopped to scoop out a handful, bringing it up to my face for a quick sniff. Then I rubbed some on my cheeks for camouflage.

The other side of the hill beckoned. Before I was halfway down I heard what sounded like someone shouting. My heart pumped mightily for a second until I saw the half-naked figure of a boy about my age playing in the creek. The water was so clear I could see the brownish-green rocks on the bottom.

"Who goes there?" The voice sounded low like a frog, the slipped up high, shimmying the scale on a second's notice.

"Who wants to know?" I answered in my tough-guy talk, the voice I used for keeping bullies away. Once they saw me, though, it didn't work. At thirteen, I was scrawny, with spindly legs and arms, not an ounce of extra flesh anywhere. The boy in the creek looked to be about the same.

"King Freddy, ruler of the creek, chief of the mountain." I could see him standing, water to his mid-thigh, both hands on his hips, an Errol Flynn stance straight from that old movie, "Robin Hood."

"My name's David. I'm new to the forest." I was beginning to like the game, but I felt a little clumsy. My gang in Texas played Monopoly or poker during the summer days by the pool and I wasn't used to pretending.

"Ho, David. Why do you come to my forest?" There was no brag in his claim, just a simple fact. He was the only one in the forest so it had to belong to him.

I was feeling brave. "I come to serve King Freddy, for I am a knight of the highest order."

"Then step forward and you shall receive my token of friendship." I half ran, half slid to meet him. Face to face, with only the water between us, I could see orange hair, a tan face and body, bright green eyes rimmed with almost white eyelashes. Circling his neck was a ring of soda pop tabs bent over on each other to make a necklace. Three bird feathers jutted out from his piece of jewelry at odd angles, one red, the other two black. This King Freddy had a regal bearing and I immediately knelt on one knee and bowed my head.

"Sir David, First Friend of the King, I command you rise, enter the sacred river and receive the ring of friendship."

I wasn't sure about entering the "sacred river." I knew Mom would kill me if I came home with wet shoes, so I took them off, then dipped my toe into the clear water. I didn't want to go on, but I looked at Freddy. He waited and I could see that his cutoffs were soaked. If he could take the cold, then I could, too. I gingerly picked my way to him. When I was within reach, he grabbed my hand, removed one of the tabs from his necklace and put it on my finger.

From that moment Freddy and I were inseparable. He taught me which vines were safe to swing from, how to catch a crawdad without getting pinched, where to find the twisted root of the ginseng, and how to get the best price for it in town. I taught him Monopoly and let him ride my bike. Best of all, he told me stories about King Arthur and the Knights of the Round Table. He'd read THE ONCE AND FUTURE KING that year in school and checked out IDYLLS OF THE KING on his own. Fighting dragons and saving damsels had become his favorite pastime and I was lucky enough to be included, lucky enough to be his right-hand man. I loved him, pure and true, the way a boy of thirteen can. But now, if I'm honest, the thing I loved most about Freddy was his mama.

What You Long For

It took Freddy almost a month to invite me to his house. Before my first visit, he made me take a blood oath that I wouldn't hold his mama against him. I didn't understand what he was talking about, but I slit the tip of my finger and meshed my blood with his anyway.

He'd asked me to spend the night. My parents were glad I'd made a friend, glad I seemed to be adjusting to the cool, humid air of West Virginia. And though my own mother worried about Freddy, who came to our house without shoes and wearing the same dirt-caked jeans, she liked him and could see the goodness of his character. That, plus the fact that he ate her cooking with a gusto her own family lacked, endeared him to her.

Freddy's house wasn't what I'd expected. I figured he lived in a three-bedroom ranch like mine. But his place was deep into the forest, about three miles from the creek where we'd met. It was an old mobile home, shorter that the ones you see now and more than a little rusty. The yard was cluttered with a large washtub, a clothes tree, and a run-down red Studebaker Lark. And lying in the fading sun, in a two-piece bathing suit with the back of the top part unhooked, was Freddy's mama. I noticed the long, tan stretch of her back and on her left shoulder blade a tiny tattoo. I'd never seen anyone with a tattoo before; not even the men at the mine where Dad worked, though some of them looked like they could have had one. Hers was a yellow butterfly and the most beautiful thing I'd ever seen.

But to say she was beautiful wouldn't cover it. She was like a movie star or one of those Amazon women I'd read about. Her hair fell across her shoulders and I haven't seen hair that color since. It was gold, a deep rich shade, until the sunlight hit it. Then it turned dark copper, the color of flame in Autumn. I wanted to touch it, twist it in my hands. I thought I could smell coconuts and I knew, somehow, that the sweetness was her natural scent. Then I realized I'd caught a whiff of her suntan lotion. It didn't matter. It might as well have been some fine perfume. On her, anything became wonderful.

When she turned to face us, I couldn't believe how young she looked. My own mother was beginning to gray and had that comfortable, lumpy look like moms are supposed to have. But Freddy's mama resembled the high school girls who sometimes rode the bus back in Texas. Her face was unlined and even without makeup her lips were filled with red. The same green eyes that lit Freddy's face were hers also, except on her they were wide and innocent, with dark lashes that flashed when she lowered them. Her figure was fit and trim, with little round breasts that nudged at her bathing suit top. She smiled at us and I felt like the world had been in an eclipse until that moment.

That night, we ate pork and beans from a can, heated over a campfire. She opened up a bag of marshmallows and taught me how to scorch the outside until it's a black crisp, then suck out the gooey white middles. After it got dark and the fire was nothing but coals, we went inside the trailer and crawled into our beds. Freddy's mama popped open a bottle of beer and offered me some. I took my first gulps and burped real loud. My face got hot but she and Freddy just laughed.

"Enough for you, Sir David. This mead's a bit strong for so gallant a warrior." She was used to Freddy's Round Table talk and often joined in.

After she and Freddy finished off the beer, she told us ghost stories, tales that would scare the pants off a grown-up. But somehow, Freddy and I weren't afraid, cuddled up in the top bunk. We grabbed each other's hands at the spookiest parts and I didn't think a thing about it although I'd have never done that with my old pals from Texas. But they hadn't heard stories like that either. Freddy's mama kept talking to us like we were somebody special.

After that, I tried to spend as many nights as I could over at Freddy's. Of course, my mom insisted that Freddy stay at our house, too and we played a thousand games of Monopoly that summer, with my dad eagerly snatching up Boardwalk and my mom landing over and over in jail. It was quiet play, the only kind allowed at my house and I soon hated the silence that would wrap around us. Freddy didn't seem to mind, though. Didn't even laugh when I called it "Monotony" as my parents set up the card table and popped popcorn and made syrupy sweet lemonade.

Freddy's place was different, each time a surprise. His mama always drank beer. Sometimes, late at night after she'd passed out on the couch, Freddy and I would sneak out. One night we saw a hoot owl on the limb of a hemlock tree, his golden eyes glowering at us, a thing possessed. Another night we spotted a herd of deer, the big buck silhouetted against the dark heavens, his crown of antlers a prize for any hunter. And once, after a long walk through an uncharted wood, we crept close enough to a fox to almost touch its tail before it ran into the underbrush.

Other times, Freddy's mama would chase us into the trees, hide and seek, then fix us hot toddies. I developed a love for the sweet taste of rum that summer. Once, at sundown, I fell from a branch midway up a tall oak. My elbow was cut, bleeding. I ran to Freddy's mama, hoping for some Bactine and a Band-Aid, my mom's favorite treatment. Freddy's mama took one look at the elbow and stared deep into my eyes.

"Sir David, this wound looks like it needs the true healing of Merlin. Come to the house." She took my earlobe and pulled gently, pinching a little, but not enough to really hurt me. The pain in my elbow grew less severe. When we arrived at the kitchen sink, she poured the rest of her beer over the cut.

"Now I'm gonna work some magic. I learned this from an old Indian wizard." She began making strange sounds and slowly rubbing her fingers up and down my arm. The song sounded like a slow version of "Sixteen Tons", but I didn't mention that. The weird thing was, it worked. I didn't tell her right away that I was feeling better. I like the sound of her voice moving over me and the touch of her fingertips.

"You sing real good." I looked at my elbow. I didn't want her to see how it scared me to say stuff like that.

"Thanks. I wanted to be a country singer. Like Loretta Lynn. Reckon I know enough about heartbreak." She had a far away look and her green eyes had turned a dull brown.

"My arm's better. Thanks." I broke from her.

"Told you—magic!" She smiled at me.

The weekend before school was to start, Freddy and I spent the whole three days at his house. Late Saturday night, Freddy's mama and I were the only ones awake. She'd had a few and was feeling like a talk.

"Before I had little Freddy, I used to sing down at The Broken Wheel. That's where I met Freddy's daddy." She leaned her head against her arm.

I didn't know she'd ever done any real singing and I'd never laid eyes on Freddy's daddy. Guess I never thought about him having one.

"Why don't you sing now? I bet you still could if you wanted to." I could see she was sad and I'd have said anything to cheer her up.

"Too late. I'm old and worn out. Waiting tables every morning grinds a person down." She looked at me a long time, then took her hand and patted me on the shoulder. All of a sudden, I knew what I had to do, what any gallant knight would do.

"I think you're the prettiest lady I ever saw!" My words came out in a sputter. I wasn't sure what to do once they'd hit the air, so I sat still and watched her. She smiled a sloppy smile.

"Why, Sir David, aren't you the sweet-talker!" Then, of all things, she leaned across the table, put her red lips to mine and kissed me. It was a real kiss, didn't last a second, but long enough. My lips tingled for days afterwards.

That Sunday, when Freddy and I got home from church (my parents always made sure I went to Sunday School, no matter where I spent the night) Freddy's mama wasn't at home. No note, no mama. We played, defended the creek from the evil emperor, caught several butterflies and let them go. Soon, the Autumn sun sank behind the mountain. We opened a can of spaghetti and warmed it, slurping the noodles with gusto, seeing who could slurp one up the fastest. It got dark suddenly, the way it does in late summer, with the night sneaking up on you while you're getting in that last hour of play. I didn't want to leave Freddy alone, but I knew I'd better get home soon. Just when I was about to invite him over, we heard the old Lark chug-a-lugging up the narrow road.

Freddy's mama was driving and she had a bright yellow scarf tied on her head. She looked kind of funny as she bustled into the trailer, hugged each of us, then took the last six-pack from under the sink, opened every can and poured it down the drain. Freddy and I sat there, immobile as two chess pieces. Then, she jerked the scarf from her head in a grand flourish.

Her hair was cut short, no more than an inch long all over. I couldn't move. I'd never seen anything like it. That short hair, and yet in the evening light, she was as pretty as ever. She began to laugh.

"Boys! Say something! Come on, speak." She cajoled us the way she always did.

Freddy was the first to reply.

"Mama, what in the hell have you done?"

"It's a Pixie cut. The latest style, honey. I'm going to make our fortune. You wait and see." She held Freddy's chin in her hand, the long red nails glossy with new polish.

"Why'd you do it?" His words were garbled, like he carried a bag of marbles in his mouth.

"I had to, baby. I couldn't think straight with it hanging all over the place." She rubbed her hands over the top of her head, pushing what was left of her hair up so that it stood erect, sort of like my dad's crewcut. Her gold earrings hung against her neck, the neck I hadn't seen before. The pale white of her skin and the graceful arch of her throat as she smiled expectantly at us made me ache for something I couldn't name.

She continued in a soft voice. "I was tired of the men at the restaurant always touching it. I don't have time to be bothered with them. I gotta write music. This is just the first step."

Freddy looked at me like what-could-be-next. I shrugged my shoulders. Freddy's mama kept babbling away, not noticing our silence.

"Freddy, honey, we're goin to Nashville." Freddy rolled his eyes. I figured it was time for me to leave.

"Sir David, I owe it all to you. You and your sweet-talking ways." She grinned at me and my lips started to feel funny.

"When I'm famous, you can visit and we'll keep you in style." I kept staring at her hair. She frowned, mocking me. "Don't look so glum—it'll grow back fast. By the time I'm ready for it, I'll have all the hair I need." Her eyes were bright with a strange quality, like there was a light behind them turning them a pale green, the color of early Spring willow leaves.

"That'll be great." My voice was flat. I looked over at Freddy. He was still staring at his mother. I slipped out the door leaving the two of them locked in silence.

I kept straight to the path, arrived home too late for supper. My mom made me bathe and iron my slacks for school the next day. It was part of her new thing—preparing me to be a bachelor. I wasn't looking forward to meeting a bunch of new kids at the bus stop the next morning, but things got better when Mom agreed that I could go to Freddy's and catch the bus with him.

The next morning I got up early, a strange excitement goading me awake. Mom hadn't awakened yet, so I knew it was early. Her alarm was set for 7 a.m. I slipped on my clothes, remembered to brush my teeth and comb my hair, then crept out the back door. I wanted to spend as much time with Freddy as possible.

I heard it a good quarter mile away from Freddy's. Mixed with the smell of bacon, it was a lush, low sound, smooth as butter, almost liquid the way it glided over notes, dipping and swaying to a rhythm that spoke to my blood. I tiptoed my way to the trailer window, took a peek inside.

Freddy's mama sat at the kitchen table, a beat-up guitar in her lap, coffee cup at her elbow. I could see where she'd scribbled something on a napkin, torn it up, then sketched it again. The song she was singing sounded sad, like the hooting of a lonely owl. It was the most haunting sound I've ever heard and I knew I was in love with her, in love with the way she looked, the way she laughed. And I knew I'd be losing her, had lost her already.

I couldn't see Freddy that morning, didn't want to face him with his mama so much on my mind. Yet I wasn't ready to leave either, so I stood outside her window as the dew hung heavy on the pines, stood so still my legs went numb, until it was time for Freddy to come out.

Before he hit the door, I ran toward home, unable to look behind me. Their bags were packed. I'd seen the big suitcase opened up across her bed. They'd be moving south soon to Nashville. Headed for adventure, for fame. Without me.

No, I couldn't talk just then. So I ran, hands over my ears, legs pumping hard, as I heard Freddy call my name.

PRODUCE

Lettyce was almost in reach of a fine red pepper when a brown arm brushed past her from behind and grabbed the very vegetable she had in her scope. She turned to find a small-boned man crowding in on her, the pepper perched like a jewel in his open palm.

"Perfect, eh?" the man said, his brown eyes almost leering at her. He had a foreign accent, but she wasn't sure where he might be from, perhaps India or Pakistan, Morocco or Persia. He was dark and the white shirt he wore was see-through. He smelled like garlic mixed with some other, more exotic odor. A sheen of perspiration covered his face like a veil.

"Yes."

Lettyce made the mistake of looking directly into his dark eyes, which were the color of freshly dug potatoes when they first come from the earth, a moist, rich shade. He held her stare for much longer than was normal. An American man would never lock eyes like that unless you were in bed with him, or planning to go to bed with him. But this man, this small-boned gentleman of indeterminate age, this man wasn't afraid to see her as she was—a middle-aged white woman in search of health foods, vegetables and fruits that might help her husband return to himself. The moment she thought of her husband, she was reminded of the sickly shade of gray his skin had become, especially when compared to the dark man who stood in front of her, still holding the firm pepper in his palm.

"For you," he said and placed the vegetable into her hand, the hand he now grasped in his own. He pressed the pepper deeply into her palm while continuing to gaze at her. She looked away, focused on the floor, then on his shoes. Loafers, soft-looking leather with scuff marks that had been polished over and over by a diligent someone who had tried hard to erase the worn look from them. He was still holding her hand, the pepper smooth and cool against her open fingers.

"No, I couldn't," she said, barely able to form the words. Her entire mouth seemed swollen, her tongue rubbery. She wondered if she were allergic to something about him.

"But you must," he said. He continued to press the pepper into her hand. She wrapped her fingers around it and put it in her cart next to the cantaloupe.

"Now, you come with me." He guided her elbow as she pushed the cart. Her legs went wobbly. She felt as if she were walking in some new atmosphere where the air was thicker, and the gravity pulled even more strongly than here, on Earth.

He led her toward the mangoes and star fruit, papayas and fresh figs. She rarely allowed herself to look at these items—she knew she couldn't afford them and even if she could, she wasn't sure how to prepare and serve them. And her husband, sick as he was, could always tell when she'd made a little splurge. Money and how she spent it had become one thing Lettyce's husband could wrap his mind around. If he weren't worried about how they were going to live on their disability income, he'd focus on the constant pain in his back that felt as if "a hot poker" were stabbing him.

Lettyce knew all the shades of his pain, all the descriptions. She no longer listened as he detailed the angst that bunched his muscles. She turned her mind to her weekly trips to the grocer's, her secret rendezvous with cabbage and kale, her clandestine meetings with the fruits of the season.

The little brown man, for that's the way Lettyce now thought of him, cradled an ugly fruit in his hands and lifted it to Lettyce's nose. The fragrance was heady and before she could stop him, he'd placed the fruit next into her basket. Then he gingerly picked up a pear-apple from the shelf, its white Styrofoam bed snug against the curve of the fruit. Again, he held it to her nose, allowed her a deep sniff, then put the pear-apple in her buggy. The man didn't speak and neither did Lettyce.

She lost track of time. The icy lights of the grocery store made it impossible to tell night from day, early morning from mid-afternoon. There were few shoppers and the ones Lettyce did see seemed to be in a fog themselves. No one spoke except for the little brown man who continued to pile her cart with fruits and vegetables, many she'd never seen before.

She didn't have any idea why she was allowing the little brown man to pull her cart, fill it with things she'd dreamed of buying. With each item, he would select the most luscious, colorful of its kind, hold it up for her inspection, insist she smell each vegetable, then gently set it in her basket. For some reason, she couldn't refuse him. It was as if he knew her, knew her in the deepest way. And he wanted to please her. This, she couldn't resist.

As they strolled up the magazine aisle, Lettyce stopped to take a peek at the latest issue of OPRAH. She loved the way Oprah looked on each month's cover—carefree, happy, thin. She wondered how Oprah managed to seem thin on the magazine cover, yet on TV she was much larger. Maybe it was true what she'd heard in her teenaged years- the camera adds at least fifteen pounds. But that wouldn't explain the big O photo on the cover. Maybe Oprah had a special camera that removed fifteen pounds.

When Lettyce looked up to see what the little brown man was picking out for her from the nearby organic fruits section, she was surprised to find he'd disappeared.

At first, she simply stood her ground. He would come back; he must. He wouldn't leave her, not now, not after he'd given her so much. But he didn't return. She wheeled through every aisle in the store, twice. He was gone.

Lettyce rolled her cart to the checkout and unloaded her beautiful foods.

"Have you seen a man…a smallish man with dark eyes?" She stammered a bit, not quite sure what to say, thrown off by the sound of her own voice, its sudden loudness.

"No. You lose somebody?" the woman answered.

"Not exactly. But do you know if he comes here often? He's a small man, foreign. Could be Indian or from the Middle East. I'm not sure."

"I just been working here three days. Ain't seen anybody like that, but then, I don't know the regulars yet," the cashier said.

"Oh."

Lettyce paid her bill, a whopping $76.89. Her husband would wonder how she could have spent so much on just the two of them. He'd demand an explanation. Maybe she could sneak in without waking him, hide the most expensive items in the back of the refrigerator and lie to him about what she'd bought. She hated lying but it was the best plan she could devise.

She drove home, hoping her husband's car would be gone, praying he'd decided to go out, get some sunshine, anything. But no, the 1989 Plymouth Acclaim was tucked beneath the carport, as usual. He hadn't stepped out of the house since his injury, at least not alone. Sometimes, he'd insist she go with him to Blockbuster for movies; occasionally, he'd accompany her to the grocery store.

She carried the four plastic sacks into the kitchen, calling out, "I'm home" as she hurried to place the items before he could discover her extravagance. She heard the television blaring from their bedroom and relaxed a little. Her husband rarely offered to help put away food if he were watching TV.

After Lettyce had hidden the food in the various compartments, she noticed the time—almost six, time to fix supper. She selected several pieces of fruit and began to make a salad. She boldly sliced the star fruit and admired its delicate shape and sweetly citrus aroma. She brought out the pear apple, removed it from its Styrofoam cradle, washed it, then cut a wedge. Juice flowed and she lapped it as it ran from her wrists. The juice was sweet and copious. Then she added chunks of red delicious apples. She sprinkled pecan pieces into the mix and finished it off with fresh pineapple pieces. The salad was fit for royalty.

"What's this?" her husband asked as he ambled into the kitchen.

"Fruit salad. I thought it'd be a nice change. Wash up, we're ready to eat," she said.

She set the table quickly, brought the large bowl of fruit into the breakfast nook and placed it near her husband's plate. She then carried tuna salad from the refrigerator and set it next to the fruit.

"Looks might fancy. You win the lottery or something?" her husband said as he sat down.

"It's just fruit."

The rest of the meal passed in silence except for her husband's occasional question about what the hell kind of fruit was this anyway. While Lettyce watched her husband chew his food, she thought of the man from the grocery store and she couldn't believe she'd allowed him to take control of her buggy like that. She vowed then and there never to do such a thing again.

As the days passed, Lettyce thought of the little brown man at the oddest moments—when she was running her bath water; during her morning showers when the water steamed up her bath and cleared her sinuses. Once, right before she drifted off to sleep, she pictured the little brown man's face just inches away from her own. In her mind, she whispered, "Who are you?"

"I am the Lover of Women," he replied.

"The Lover of Women?" Lettyce said.

"Yes. I am the Lover of Women and I come to those who need me. When you see a gray-haired woman in a wheelchair, seemingly in another world, she is with me. For the middle-aged blond whose beauty is fading, I come. For the widow woman, it is I who help her through the nights of loneliness. I am the Lover of Women."

Lettyce opened her eyes and sat up in the bed. The man's voice had sounded so real, so amazingly real that she had to be certain he wasn't in the room with her.

"Can't sleep?" her husband mumbled and turned his back to her.

"Thought I heard something. But it's nothing. Sorry," she said as she stared into the darkness.

Lettyce drove by the grocery the next day, but she couldn't make herself get out of the car. After all, she had no need of anything. She felt silly cruising the parking lot of the Piggly Wiggly looking for the little brown man, a.k.a. the 'Lover of Women.' She shook her head, smiled at herself and turned the wheel, heading toward the coffee shop where she was supposed to meet her next-door neighbor, part of her weekly ritual for getting out of the house and away from her husband.

Two weeks passed before Lettyce was forced to return to the store. Her husband needed new razor blades and had started complaining about the weird suppers she'd been preparing—ham and eggs one night, pancakes the next, cold cereal after that. She'd been avoiding the store, but she could see she couldn't put off her shopping any longer. She swept past the automatic doors, grabbed a cart and hurried to the frozen foods. She was peering at Haagen Daas, imagining the smooth taste of coffee ice cream melting down her throat, when she felt a sudden presence. She turned to see the little brown man placing a pint of rum raisin in her cart.

"Oh...I couldn't..." she said, her face growing warm.

"Not so good as coffee, but still...," he replied.

"How did you know coffee's my favorite?" she said.

"I know very much from your eyes, the light in them. I can read it. Come." He took hold of her elbow with one hand and pushed the cart with the other. He led her to the cookies.

"I don't buy cookies. I'm watching my weight," Lettyce whispered to him as he piled two bags of Pepperidge Farm Chocolate Chunk Cookies into her buggy.

"You are perfect. You look as a woman of your age should look. You are not a girl anymore. You are a woman. Be a woman," he said.

Again, he took her elbow. This time, he used the buggy to force open the steel doors that said 'Employees Only.'

"Where are you going? We're not supposed to be in here," Lettyce said as they entered the dark warehouse area. Crates of bananas were stacked against one well. Empty boxes littered the others. A few scattered vegetable parts were strewn across the floor—celery stalks, carrot tops, a mushy tomato. The air smelled fruity, almost too sweet like an apple just before it goes too far.

"Who are you?" Lettyce could barely get the words out. She looked hard at him but he seemed to blend into the shadows. Her eyes hadn't yet adjusted to the cave-like light.

"Who are you?" His voice seemed to come from all around her.

What You Long For

"You're scaring me. I'm leaving." Lettyce didn't move.

"No. Please. Stay."

She felt something cool brush against her neck and she saw that he had moved behind her. His hands were on her waist and she could feel the warmth of his whole body as he stood there, steady. Without thinking, she leaned into him. He removed his hands from her waist and began working with something. She didn't watch what he was doing. Instead, she rolled her head back against him. He was shorter than she and she could feel his lips moving on her neck as he spoke.

"Yes. Now you are a woman. Now you are as you should be."

She smelled the sudden tangy scent of a tangerine, then felt cool juice drip onto the space between her collar bones. His hands squeezed one section of the tangerine, then another. He rubbed the juice into her chest.

The juice felt cool and the sharp scent made her scalp tingle in a strange way. The little brown man was massaging her chest, her breasts. Her nipples drew into hard little gumdrops and she stood in a daze while the man gently pinched them and sucked at them with his palms.

"Relax. This, this is what you long for, no?"

His voice had become mellow and smooth, a thick syrup. She didn't move, though somewhere her mind was telling her to shake free from this strange man and his heavenly hands. He continued to touch her shoulders, her chest, her neck until she thought she might simply die right there in the supermarket storage area.

Then, without warning, he stopped.

Lettyce felt him gently tug at her elbow and guide her toward the double doors, back into the fluorescent lights of the dairy aisle. Obediently, she entered by the skim milk and watched as he put a pint of whipping cream into her cart.

"Tonight, use this for dessert. You will think of me," he said and stared up at her with his potato-colored eyes.

She shook her head, closed her eyes. She was going to tell him that what they were doing was dangerous. She was going to tell him she was a married woman, too old for this sort of thing. She was going to tell him she might even report him to the manager but when she opened her eyes, he was gone. Just like that. Without a trace.

Again, she scoured the store, asking a young mother with two toddlers if she'd seen the little man. An old man with a crumpled hat said he might have seen someone scooting out the door but he couldn't be sure. No one seemed to know anything.

As Lettyce pushed her cart through the automatic doors, she noticed a woman about her age standing at the edge of the sidewalk, shielding her eyes from the sun. The woman's gaze was intent on something and Lettyce was reluctant to disturb her.

"Excuse me. I was wondering if you've seen a man just now. He's short, around 5'5" and slim. Indian or something," Lettyce said.

"No. No. No one like that," the woman sputtered, her cheeks flushed and her blue eyes moist. She continued to stare into the half-full lot.

"Well, thanks," said Lettyce.

That night, after she'd covered a strawberry shortcake with the whipped cream the little man had forced into her cart, Lettyce dreamed. In her dream, she was naked and surrounded by fruit, strange, animal-like fruit that walked and wiggled its way to where she lay stretched out on a fluffy, red beach towel. A mobile mango slithered onto her big toe and began to squeeze itself to death while the juice ran, sticky and sweet, into the hot sands of what she thought must have been Monte Carlo. Then, before her eyes, what looked like a misshapen Bartlett pear rolled onto her belly and slowly, ever so slowly moved back and forth between her navel and the first hint of her pubic hair. In her dream, she was young and luscious and her veins were filled with golden blood, thick as honey.

When she awoke the next morning, she felt as though the world had turned, the slant of its axis slightly askew.

Lettyce hadn't been to the store in three weeks, the longest she'd ever gone without shopping for food. She'd vowed not to set foot in the Piggly Wiggly until she could be sure the strange little man wouldn't be there. She'd used all her frozen meat, hard round blobs of mysterious stuff that revealed itself after a few minutes in the microwave. And she'd even cooked the fish her husband had caught, how long ago was it? She was afraid to remember for fear of food poisoning, yet she'd deep-fried the filets all the same. Luckily, no one got sick and she was spared a grocery run.

You might wonder why Lettyce didn't simply shop at a different supermarket. After all, a Harris Teeter perched on the corner near her subdivision, a Food Lion just a few miles beyond the Harris Teeter. Why was Lettyce faithful to her Piggly Wiggly?

The truth? Lettyce wanted to see the man again. She wanted him to place items in her buggy and make her dream of animated apples and garrulous grapes. She was teasing him, that's all. Making him want her, want her, want her.

Lettyce ran her finger down the rind of an almost overripe cantaloupe, then tapped it twice. The sweet, sharp smell of fruit and earth shook loose and Lettyce smiled, scooped the melon up in both hands and carefully placed it in her shopping cart, in the small section set up for children. She patted the cantaloupe carefully, as if it were, indeed, a toddler. She then rolled on toward the spinach and peppers, the yellow and red ones her favorites. Soft rock music from the Sixties played over the store's intercom and Lettyce became conscious that she was still smiling in a strange, hopeful way.

She'd seen no sign of the little brown man and this was her second trip to the Piggly Wiggly in a week. Part of her was disappointed that he hadn't been there; the other part relieved. Lettyce rolled past the fresh produce section and was just about to place a bag of oranges into the cart when she felt a hand firmly on her waist.

"You have missed me, no?" a voice whispered close to her ear.

She turned to face him and was surprised at how small he seemed. His head barely came to her chin. His hair, thick and streaked with gray, gave off a delicate aroma that reminded her of apple blossoms, the kind she's had in her front yard when she was a girl.

"Yes, I have," she said, her voice also a whisper. She couldn't believe she'd admitted to him that she'd thought of him, longed for his touch. And tangerines. She thought she'd tell him to leave her alone, to get out of her way before she called the store manager. But instead, she confessed her desire to see him.

"Come."

He guided her, his hand on the curve of her waistline, firm pressure against her lower back. Again, they glided past the steel doors marked 'Employees Only' and entered the dark world of boxed vegetables and fruit. His first move was to lean her back against a box of oranges fresh from Florida. The oranges made a fairly soft cushion and felt like some sort of exotic massage against her back, rolling and pushing here, then here. The little man had lifted her skirt and was placing strawberries across her lower abdomen. He then began to nibble them slowly, one at a time, while juice ran down his chin and onto her belly. She could feel some of the juice dribble between her legs. His hands began to touch her. It seemed his hands flew everywhere, even to places where her husband hadn't dared.

A flash of light. A deep throbbing that shuddered from her belly to her groin to her feet, then up through her head.

What You Long For

She couldn't breathe, couldn't think. Finally, after what seemed like several minutes, her thoughts came again and she panted, the lumpy oranges no longer comfortable but now hard and unforgiving.

"Who are you?" Lettyce asked again.

"You know who I am. I am who I said I was," the little man answered, his hand still on her lower abdomen, his fingers slowly touching the crease between her leg and body.

Lettyce didn't move but allowed his fingers their play. Again and again, she trembled with pleasure until she simply couldn't bear any more. She struggled to get up, pulled her skirt back down and turned to adjust her panties in a sudden rush of modesty. When she turned back around, the little man was gone. Lettyce straightened her hair, dabbed at the juice running down her legs with a Kleenex from her purse. She then pushed the cart out of the back room into the bright lights of the Piggly Wiggly. The only other person she noticed was an old woman standing next to the boxed candy, just standing there still as death.

Lettyce started to turn her cart in the other direction, knowing she'd return again and again to the Piggly Wiggly, knowing she would meet the Lover of Women many times. She looked once more at the silent, gray-haired woman whose mouth was open slightly, her eyes unfocused and wild-looking. Lettyce smiled and wondered what the Lover of Women looked like for that old lady. It didn't matter. Suddenly, nothing mattered—not her husband's clammy skin, his whining complaints; not her own body, sagging and shrinking.

The Lover of Women would fix everything.

DICKHEAD

Yeah, that's right—I'm a dick, a rod, a cock, a dorkle, a prick, a pecker, a pole, a sword, a trouser-snake, a joystick—the old one-eyed, purple-headed monster. And I'm telling it like it is, here at the center of the universe, right in the middle of the BVD's. Hell, they got the Vagina Monologues; I figured it was only fair to me to have a say. Nobody thinks I've got much on my mind except a good fuck. But nobody would be wrong. Contrary to popular opinion, I got a lot to talk about; I'd like to see you try to stop me.

First, you got to understand a few things. Me and him—you know, the dude I'm attached to—sometimes we're connected and sometimes, well, we ain't. I see the same stuff he sees, but I go my own way and he goes his. It's weird, I know. But hey, not my design.

Name's Old Faithful. His woman gave me that title years ago, at least that's what she told *him* the other night while she was trying to make him feel better about Their Problem. Said she could always count on me, depended on me really. *He* never called me much of nothing except Big Buddy. Every once in a while, he'd shout my full name, though—

Great God Almighty! I don't blame him for not addressing me with the whole shebang all the time—that's a big name to spew out every time he talked to me. And he does yak. He's like a super cheerleader or something. "Come on, Big Buddy! Get going, Big Buddy!" All that talking and thinking hard can get on a pecker's nerves.

She's been talk, talk, talking to *him* all the damn time—no wonder I'm having a problem. Told him having me around gave her a sense of power; she knew she could bring me to life whenever she wanted—at least, that was the way I used to work. Poor thing. She told him she still needed that power, especially now that her internal clock had changed and she could no longer count the gray in her hair—just too much of it. Then she started tearing up, her eyes filling and overrunning down her face. How the hell can I do what I'm supposed to when she's all smeary with crying? I mean, I ain't exactly young myself and she's putting the pressure on me big-time.

I remembered then how she used to coax me along sometimes. Oh, I always liked her coaxing. Sometimes, she'd cover me with food—syrup, honey, cream, even sugar. I wasn't too crazy about the sugar but in the end, she made everything fine.

He's a damn fool, though. Won't talk to her about me. Refuses to explain how I've changed, how I can't rise to the occasion the way I once did, since he hurt his back three summers ago painting the house. Fell off the ladder, wouldn't you know it. Busted up a bunch of disks. Since then, he doesn't talk to her much. And when she comes to him smelling all lemony like heavy flowers in August, he tells her he's tired. Or turns away from her like he doesn't care what she smells like.

Fucking liar. Yeah, that's what he is. He never tells her that he still dreams of her, of the two of them. How in his dreams, they are both as they were before, her all silky and moist; me, lean and, well, hard. He never tells her how damn depressed he is about Their Problem, how he can't stop thinking about it, how he's scared shitless she'll leave him.

Fucking liar and coward, to boot.

She told him the other day how I didn't really matter to her. Can you believe that shit? Told him what she wanted was to feel his body naked against her own. She told him she wanted him to look at her, see her, the whole of her, spirit and body and heart and soul. She told him she wanted *him* to make love to all of that. And *he* couldn't use me, no matter what. I was okay with that, believe it or not. I mean, no pressure—maybe something could happen.

You know what that stupid fucker did?

"I don't see the point in that." (Didn't I tell you *he* was a dumbass?)

But she didn't give up. She said, "The point is for us to connect—be intimate. I don't care about genitals being involved. We can find other ways… ." (See how she is? Man, I was so ready to do anything she said, even though I lay there like a dead fish.)

"Well, I care." (Then the dumb fuck turned over and pretended to go to sleep. He didn't fool her, though. I could hear her crying on her side of the bed. I tried to send him a message—go to her, go to her, dammit! But he wouldn't budge, not one inch.)

I tried then, struggled with all I could muster. I wanted to rise up, just like Jesus from the tomb. And in my rising, I would reach out to her and give her comfort. I would go to that dark place I know so well, open the gate with such tenderness that she wouldn't cry anymore. Or maybe she would cry but the tears would be a cry for life, for love. And then, once I'd entered the deep cave I call home, we could begin the slow dance that takes us away from every hurt this old world can give.

Of course, that ain't what happened. I could feel myself begin to grow just a little. I was encouraged. Yeah, this was good. Then *he* got involved. He figured I wouldn't work, not really, so he told himself to go to sleep. It wasn't worth risking another failure. He couldn't take another failure.

Man, if he'd just let me alone, I think I coulda done okay. But no, he's the boss. Wasn't so long ago, I was the boss myself. Where I went, he followed. Now, he's in charge and he's a fucking idiot. Okay, he's not a *fucking* idiot.

You know, things aren't all that bad. I mean, I can think a little now, consider the big questions. I know, I know—nobody believes I have a brain. I admit, it ain't much but I haven't exactly exercised it over the years. I thought about nothing but my prime purpose all the time—and I do mean ALL THE TIME.

I could say I don't miss being my old self too much. But that's bullshit. I miss it like crazy. Especially when *he* sees her, sometimes, while she's busy around the house. Or when he sees her holding the grandbaby. Something comes over her then and he remembers her holding our babies, nestling them to her breasts, the same breasts I love to this day. Her face is sort of radiant and her voice softens to a low cooing sound. I've heard that sound before. It's the same one she makes when I enter her.

Or should I say when I entered her. Seems past tense makes more sense.

I know what you're thinking. Why doesn't *he* take that Viagra shit? Sad to say, the pills don't work for me. With nerve damage, pills are useless. You'd think Dickhead would try to find other ways, but *he's* still so sore about the whole business, he'd rather I shrink up and die than ask anyone for help. I mean, if he asked somebody, then that somebody would know.

Know what? I want to ask *him*. That you're human? That you're not as young as you used to be? That you have fallen to the ravages of time as every man alive will at some point?

He doesn't listen to me. He doesn't listen to her. He just acts like nothing's wrong and sleeps as close to the edge of his side of the bed as possible.

Jerk.

But wait. What's this? Here we are, sleeping late on a Saturday morning. We can hear the birds outside the open window. It's spring and the air is fresh and cool. He's looking at her as she emerges from her shower. (Hell, I hadn't even heard her get out of bed but damn, she looks good!)

She's wrapped in a towel with a turban on her head. He can see the beads of water on her legs (still sexy, still make me think of them circling him around the waist while I'm busy inside her) and her face is without makeup. She's pretty, her green eyes filled with the morning light, a strand of wet hair curling down her cheek. She smiles at him and puts something that smells like oranges and ginger on her arms, legs, now on her belly. Her towel has fallen away.

He can see stretch marks across her stomach, trails of her sons coming into this world. She told *him* once that even if they could afford it, she'd never have a tummy tuck, never remove those traces of the nest she once was. I loved it when she said that.

He's looking at her now and thank God, he's not thinking anything. He's just watching her, and somehow, I am, too. See how her skin glistens. How her body is soft and warm. See how she looks at *him*, her eyes full of something fresh, hopeful. See the curve of her breast, the nipple erect in the morning air. See. ... See. ...

NAMESAKE

Funny about names. You might guess that my great uncle Edwin was a lifelong bachelor with thin, narrow shoulders and close-set eyes that pinched together when he tallied his ledgers. And you'd be right, of course. That's exactly what an Edwin would look like.

Change but a few letters and you alter a man forever. An -ard instead of the -in at the end of his moniker would have given my uncle a kingly name—Edward. Legs thick and steady at the bow of a ship, well-muscled arms guiding the wheel. Even the rough seas would not stir such a man and dark thunderclouds would find a permanent home in his eyes.

Rather than captain ships, Uncle Edwin built them. More specifically, he owned a company in Boston that manufactured vessels for the United States Navy during the War Between the States. It's unlikely that Uncle Edwin could have managed to nail one plank aboard the bow, but he knew how to run a profitable business and exact an honest day's work for little pay.

Yes, my uncle fit his nomenclature and died of consumption in mid-life, at the beginning of the last decade of the last century, the Nineteenth. How antiquated that sounds! Not modern like our new Twentieth, with its automobiles and electricity. Though I was born in the late 1800's, I welcome the promises held in the word 'twentieth,' a coming of age for the whole world. And to carry me into that fashionable time, I've a small share of Uncle Edward's money.

His nest egg, for so he always called it, was much larger than the phrase implies, and came to my father, Wallace, a greedy name which didn't fit the mild-mannered parent whose pale features I inherited.

My name is Edwina, after my uncle, who hoarded his money, neither marrying nor giving a dollar to nieces and nephews on holidays. At his death, his detailed instructions for an ostentatious funeral were carried out to the letter by my father, who seemed quite embarrassed by the entire event. A church full of flowers and not a soul there for the service, except, of course, our little family, Mother, Father, my brother, George, and myself.

Father, finding himself not a builder of any sort, sold the company and took Mother and me to Charleston, South Carolina, where the year-round warmth soothed his joints and Mother found solace in the large Episcopal church where she sang alto in the choir. George was left in Boston, in a proper boarding school for boys his age. Mother explained such schooling was the custom among the rich and now that we could afford things, George would receive the very best. She made no mention of what I might expect.

Upon our arrival in the sun-filled South, I, Edwina, took to considering the sounds in a name, the power you call up when you declare a thing.

My own designation is a form of the masculine, but the added syllable gives it a shrill, irritating resonance. As a result, I feel as if the name is a kind of diminutive, though I know better. I certainly feel less than a man, not as important, or as interesting. I feel less even than a narrow man like

Uncle Edwin. My hair, pulled away from my face to add a sense of fullness, is pale brown. Some call it mousy, but I prefer to say bunny brown. Rabbits are superior rodents, after all. And my eyes, by some genetic miracle the exact same shade as my hair, are too close together, shaped like small quail eggs.

Maybe not. Could be my hair is thick, raven-colored and my eyebrows spear their points into my forehead with brutal force. And my eyes. The deep, steely gray of bullets circled by a darker ring around the iris. A mouth, not whitish and drawn, but red and indefinite, a blood smear.

But no, you were right the first time. An Edwina couldn't be as dramatic as that. An Edwina would be a spinster and all that word implies. Nothing could grow on an Edwina, except thoughts, barbed jealousies of all the Clarissas and Juliannas that swirl across the ballroom floor while Edwina stands over the punch bowl and feigns fascination with sherbet.

An Edwina would be the butt of jokes from nasty little boys. Oh, the humiliation. The event recalled still turns my pasty face a mottled pink.

One Sunday, when I was a child of seven, we attended our first picnic at the new Episcopal church. I didn't want to play with the other children, boys mostly, already dirty from dabbing at the edge of the creek that ran by the churchyard. Mother forced me, pushing my narrow, hunched up shoulders into the sunny field crawling with the dark shapes of children.

One of the girls approached me, hesitantly asked my name. I barely whispered, "Edwina." A know-nothing boy who'd hidden behind a nearby bush, yelled at the top of his frenzied lungs "Ed-wee-wee!" The adults had, by this time, gathered around the picnic tables and were in the process of preparing the food. There was no one, not even my little brother, George, to help me.

Soon, all the wicked little boys were screeching about my name and various bodily functions. I won't repeat all that was said.

I simply stood there, motionless and silent, until the horrible monsters lost interest in plaguing me. The girls, shocked by my lack of violence against the naughty fellows who were their brothers and friends, left me alone. That was the beginning of my social life in Charleston. Oh, I did receive party invitations after the horrid event. Mother saw to that. After all, we were wealthy, even richer than the aristocracy of the South. Money can take one a long way. Perhaps not everywhere, but almost.

I knew then, at that tender age, the awesome power of language. Though words broke no bones, they could surely hurt you. And I began to dwell on my name.

Not that Edwina is the only name with its future held in the syllables. Take Jack. Jack Sprat, Jack Frost, Jack… well, decorum forbids it. Oh, Jack's the name of a rake, a rogue, a little white-headed boy with a wide grin, who'd steal your lunch the minute your back is turned.

I loved a Jack once. He stood outside the marketplace on a frosty morning. I noticed him right away, though I was supposed to be choosing the sweet potatoes for our upcoming Thanksgiving meal. Usually, the cook, Hesperus, did our marketing, but Mother always insisted that for special occasions, I would oversee Cook's business. Mother knew that anyone with a name like Hesperus couldn't be trusted on holidays.

Jack wore a blue silk cravat at his throat and his shirt had tiny tucks across the front like a wedding shirt. His suit, black and expensive, fit him well and showed off his squarish body, the thick muscled body of a fighter or a man who labored outside at a job that called for strength.

He didn't fidget but simply waited until Cook and I carried our bundles out the front door.

"'Scuse me, ma'm. You look like you might need a little help with those. May I?" He already had relieved me of my package and was in the process of claiming one of Cook's. She didn't relinquish hers so easily.

"I manage myself, thank you." Her tone asked, 'Who he think he is, talking straight out to Miss Edwina, right here on the street?' At that moment, I felt an undeniable fondness for Cook, though usually I resented our joint errands.

I stared into Jack's pure blue eyes and said, "It's all right, Cook. This gentleman only wishes to assist us and I'm sure meant no harm." I smiled at him with as much warmth as I could muster and hoped it would be enough.

Immediately, he asked my name and before I had a chance to consider, I'd blurted out the truth. An error. If only I'd answered Suzanne or Catherine, names with regal bearing and beauty. I could almost see his disappointment when my mouth formed the -weee part of the second syllable, that long E whistling across my windpipes like the screech of an unsightly starling.

When he'd given me his Jack, my heart pumped quickly. It was a fast name, one that promised adventure, maybe even danger. One beat and it was over—a single-syllable you could spit out in anger or gasp in passion. The thought made me blush and I was glad. At least I wouldn't seem so pale in the November air.

Along the several blocks to the waterfront and my home, I discovered much about my Jack.

"Where are you from, Mr. Applewhite?" His surname, not the least bit aristocratic, was so unlike my own, Carruthers, a title of bluest blood. I rather enjoyed the difference. And he was unusual as well, nothing like the slender young men I saw escorting debutantes, boys little used to physical labor, but accustomed to leisure and plenty.

"West Virginia. I'm in the coal industry. Came south on business." West Virginia was an inappropriate state, I knew, but, though his manners weren't as smooth as those of Charleston boys, he tried to show his civil acumen. Besides, his voice was so manly, a deep baritone with a bit of gravel in it, that I began to thrill to the sound and walked more closely than was quite proper. He noticed and his arm brushed mine on more than one occasion.

"How long will you be staying?" It was an innocent question, I thought. Nothing indecent about such a general interrogation.

"Several months, I hope. Long enough to become a friend to the South." He looked directly at me, as though I represented that friend he wished to make.

"Tell me, how does a lovely woman such as yourself find entertainment here?" Not a single soul had ever called me lovely before. And I knew, from hours of prayer at my looking-glass, that, indeed, I was not lovely. But hearing him say it made me hope it was true.

"Well, there are lots of parties, cotillions. And of course the symphony…" I chattered away as if I were privy to these social gatherings. Yes, I'd attended, but always in the company of my parents, never with a young man or a group of friends my own age. For a woman of twenty-five, I'm certain that must have been some kind of record.

I'll never forget the walk that day. Though it was November, the air was somewhat warm and there were a few bright leaves scattered among the tree limbs. The water, green like the underbelly of our local lizards, was calm, serene.

Or maybe the day was cold, the wind a whip to us, forcing us to huddle together. The waves rose and fell like heavy breath and before I knew it, I'd asked Sweet Jack in for some hot tea. I knew Mother would be shocked at such a brazen move on my part, but I didn't care. Nor did I mind that Jack was an outsider. It was, after all, the Twentieth Century. In 1912, an invitation to tea must be allowed. Progress, after all.

I knew what Mother would say to my arguments. "Just because things change, doesn't make forward behavior right. You'll see. Decency will always be decency."

Mother counted everything by such rules. And by names. The stores she frequented, the goods she purchased, the street she lived on-Darlington Avenue, in the heart of the wealthy section-Mother chose as a result of the name. I, too, took notice of such things, but for different reasons.

"Delighted." Mother's only comment to Jack that afternoon, delivered in a voice that predicted the cold of the coming winter.

"You have a lovely home, Mrs. Carruthers." He tried every tack the poor man's brain could think of. Nothing worked. Mother soon left us to our tea, her 'mmmm' lingering in the air, wrapping us together against the chill she left behind.

After that first day, Jack and I met frequently, always uptown. I concocted a thousand reasons to shop and Mother didn't bat an eye when I insisted on planning our menus for the Yuletide celebrations. I chose recipes clipped from the society page of our paper. These called for exotic items which Cook and I searched for relentlessly.

What Mother didn't know was that I'd leave Cook to shop while I walked down stretches of cobbled roads, mud byways, rutted routes and woodsy paths. I kept to the clean side of town at first, followed street names I knew well. Often I'd meet Jack on these thoroughfares by secret arrangement. We'd stroll together, me on important business and Jack for the pleasure of my company. So he told me.

But before I realized, I began to drift over to the other sections of town on my daily outings. The wharves and seedier places where the stench of commerce hung on the air, where everything was for sale at one price or another. The first time Jack took me to these dark, dangerous streets, I considered racing home, back to the world I knew, a world with rules. But it didn't take long for him to convince me that life held more than rules.

Once I saw a woman dressed in what must have been the most lewd underskirts I'd ever seen. She waved at Jack almost as if she knew him. He kept his eyes on me, however, and didn't seem to notice her at all. It's my belief she was a woman of ill repute. The thought excited me in a way I couldn't quite fathom. I enjoyed meandering through these low sections, safe on Jack's sturdy arm. I became an explorer of sorts, making forays into forbidden territory, the way I imagined men of Jack's caliber might venture without fear to new places.

I watched street signs, not for directions, but for clues. Regis Park had such a lovely sound, like a fine place where they served meals, even breakfast, with the good silver. In reality, the road itself was of sand and soot and my boots had to be cleaned for three hours to remove all evidence of my journey, according to Cook, who never uttered a word of complaint over her extra, clandestine duties.

Then there was Market Street, a place that implied noise and bustling business. Another lie. It was a narrow, one-lane gully that led past the stockyards to the river. As I made these discoveries, I began to look for such incongruities in human names. I'd discovered that though called 'Edwina', I had the heart of a Gwendolyn, a passionate nature that enjoyed stealing away into the nether parts of Charleston. A woman accompanied was allowed access to the entire city, where a woman alone... .well, no decent woman would stroll by herself in such places.

Sometimes on our excursions, I had hints about how I'd appear at mid-life, Edwina Carruthers, a clumsiness having taken over my youthful temerity, my gait like that of a broken mule. These visions were triggered by the sight and sound of a particularly unattractive person of mean circumstances, male or female, young or old. Then I'd force myself to consider the passion I felt, my secret 'Gwendolyn' nature. Perhaps I'd become one of those lush women, full and earthy, who are able to wear their womanhood like a mantle of ermine, soft and elegant. Or, if my name were Edwina Applewhite? The sound of it was too much to be imagined and I could get no image, none at all.

Such thoughts, dark and cloudy, didn't matter, though, because Jack would meet me and distract me from my considerations. Together we would walk in the last moments before dark, those rosy minutes when the sun hit the painted wrought iron fence behind my house and turned it a rosy vermilion.

Even my face took on the peachy glow of sunset and it was then that Jack ventured to kiss me as we stood down by the boat docks.

Or the day might have been stormy, the wind a robber stealing warmth, turning our mouths filmy with the cold. Blue-lipped, face the color of thin, gray clouds, Jack at my elbow, I was never kissed, but rather skated around the town, gliding, the hem of my dress catching on the rough sidewalk boards at the harbor.

Jack told me all about the mountains of West Virginia and how he'd become involved in the mining industry. Without actually saying so, he indicated he had attended West Point.

"I enjoyed my military service, Miss Carruthers. And, were it not for my clumsily flat feet, I might have continued it." He always called me Miss Carruthers, though he knew my given name. I knew he couldn't bear the sound of it, didn't want to assault the air with its ugly implications. And I always addressed him as Mr. Applewhite. We were, after all, not betrothed. We were walking partners.

I could see Jack in my mind's eye, crisp and starched in his uniform, the younger soldiers calling him 'sir.' Oh, how I longed to become something more to him than his South Carolina friend. How I wished to be on his arm at important gatherings, business meetings that might change the course of our very own South. I wanted to be dressed in the finest silks and satins. I could, after all, afford such luxuries. Only my linsey-woolsey name kept me from the fabrics most women of my station wore with enjoyment. After all, what would Uncle Edward have thought about such indulgences? And how could I feel the smooth fabric against my skin without flinching at the rough sound of my own name?

I knew I'd never be anything beyond Edwina for Jack. Even my middle name, Jane, wouldn't serve to distinguish me. Jack deserved an Estelle or a Colette.

Imagine my chagrin when he didn't seem to understand our obvious positions. Truth be told, I couldn't imagine myself with a Jack, no matter how bright his future looked, no matter the allure of his masculine voice. There's something missing in the name, a lack of trustworthiness that I could see for myself. I didn't need Mother's constant reminding.

"Edwina, I've discovered with whom you take your walks, my dear. I must warn you, there's something about Mr. Applewhite... the garish way his ears stick out. You can't trust a man who looks so comical from behind. I won't forbid you to see him, but I will surely disinherit you if anything untoward happens."

Where Mother saw deformity, I saw beauty. The wide expanse of cartilage between the rim of his ear and his head seemed to me the perfect place to kiss or run over with the tip of one's tongue. Such thoughts shocked me and I knew they sprang from that other nature, the Gwendolyn, a woman capable of who-knew-what. Mother's sermon didn't tell me one thing I couldn't have already guessed. Jack was so handsome, so charming, women would never leave him alone. And I sometimes doubted his purity of motive. The idea that he might be interested in me for investment purposes had occurred. But I never dwelt on it.

On the night, or was it morning, that he proposed, the moon was a sliver, a pale C against the dark heavens.

The spring night air was cool, but clear and I could see the stars, bright pinpricks of light scattered across the dusky sky. The ocean itself was subdued and quiet. We stood under the weeping willow tree in the garden behind my house. His eyes, intelligent, but gentle, seemed to plead for understanding and affection. A shock of blond hair fell across his wide forehead and there, in the late evening, he seemed to be more than he actually was—a pirate, a gambler, a spy. Unfortunately, I was exactly what I was, Edwina.

He took my gloved hand in his own squarish one, cupped it gently, like my fingers were made of porcelain. He kissed them one by one, the warmth of his lips burning through the material. His eyes didn't leave my face and I could feel myself sinking, sinking down into the mist that rose off the water. I'd give myself to him, there was not one doubt. Marry up with him, though I could see there'd be nothing but trouble. A country bumpkin really, that's all he was in spite of his varnish of etiquette. Jack Applewhite. Humph. A name common as chicken feed.

Yet, I could have taken his name, woven my initials with his on our monogrammed linens. I could have, but instead I sealed our fates.

His voice was all atremble. "Edie, would you consider marrying me?"

Edie! He'd never hinted that he thought of me that way. The huskiness of the repeated 'E' sound, low and rather desperate, made me quiver. Some force took hold of me, some ancient thing. I threw my arms around his thick neck.

"Call me Edie again. Say it, Jack, say it." The growl that tore from his throat terrified me, yet I found myself kissing him, allowing him to touch me, lift my skirts. We fell together under the willow tree, hidden from my house, Mother becoming a part of the shadows.

Or perhaps there was no riotous behavior in the darkened grass. Instead, he simply fell to one knee, tucked his hat under his arm and made his request.

"Now will you marry me, Edwina Jane Carruthers?" His voice sounded confident, a slight derisive emphasis on the last two syllables of my first name. Or so I thought. He kept talking but I didn't hear anything after he'd called me by my full name. In those few syllables, I heard my whole life pass in one long moment. Edwina Jane couldn't marry, wouldn't take a man into her bedroom. Not nightly. Not to be defiled on a regular basis. She hadn't the nerve to slip under the covers wearing no undergarments, an Edwina couldn't stand the passion of such nights. She'd burn up as quickly as pine needles in autumn. No, Edwina Jane sat alone in the library reading *Sonnets to the Portuguese*, dreaming of Robert Browning (a stalwart name), just the sort of man who might steal her away. The fire lit her white features, ruddied up her sunken cheeks and cast hints of gold in her eyes.

Edwina Jane dared not bear the consequence of children, a bloody reminder of joined names. No child would want an Edwina for a mother, a woman cold and hard, with bony places in her heart. And what family heirloom could Jack give the hybrids he might spawn? Applewhite? It sounded like a kind of whiskey.

The silence of the next few moments was loud as the squall of the sea. Jack tried to force me to look at him, but after my complete display of myself, I dared not. He kept talking, his voice sad and low. He seemed at odds, not quite knowing what to do. I stared out upon the water, said nothing, did not move, barely breathed. I lost track of time, could only note the rise of the moon as it lifted, like a sickle, across the heavens.

Finally, Jack took my arm and led me to our parlor door. I saw Mother staring out the bay window in the dining room, a gray shape behind the curtain. I continued my silence, refused to utter a word. I could hear the waves and the sound was like a voice, a soft something calling. I could only sigh and mouth "Mrs. Jack Applewhite" over and over, my face hidden under a winter bonnet, the wool of the brim sturdy against the biting wind.

Though I mouthed the words, I knew they would never become real. I would refuse Jack, had already turned against him. Any man who could sway me the way he had, who could think of me as 'Edie', such a man was dangerous.

LUCY AND ETHEL

Forty-four. Forty-four and alone. Forty-four and alone on her birthday. Husband away on business, daughter at a church lock-in. Well, Barb decided it didn't really matter. Forty-four wasn't a very important year anyway. It wasn't the Big 4-0 or the Big 5-0. It wasn't any -0- at all. Just one of those awkward in-between years.

The awkward in-between. That's what she was, all right. She chugged down the last half of her fourth wine cooler, the new flavor, Fuzzy Navel. She liked it. Sweet peach and orange mixed with some sort of white wine, she supposed. Whatever it was, the concoction hit the spot and Barb eased herself up from the kitchen table to start on the next 4-pack.

Drinking alone in her kitchen wasn't something Barb normally did. Matter of fact, she rarely took spirits, as her mother used to call anything alcoholic. Her husband teased her, called her a "cheap date" when they'd first begun seeing each other. Twenty years ago. The time had slipped through her hands like water.

And now, here she was, forty-four, the same age her mother'd been when she died.

Numbers are strange. They have their own secret code. Forty-three didn't sound old to Barb at all. It was a hopeful age, still young enough to achieve something, if Barb could figure out what it was she wanted to achieve. Still an attractive age, one where young men might turn their eyes toward her.

But forty-four was different. Though only one year older, the sound of it aged her even as she sat sucking down coolers. She was almost halfway to fifty. And everybody knew fifty was the beginning of the end. You couldn't fake anyone out when you were fifty. You'd either been successful or you hadn't. You'd stayed married or lost your husband to some young thing. Your children were on their own or camped out in their old bedrooms, still tossing dirty clothes on the bathroom floor. Yep, by fifty, the truth came home to roost. It wouldn't be put off any longer.

Barb didn't want to be bothered by the truth. She didn't want to face up to her life. Instead, she desired youth, that springy time when nothing mattered so much, when failure meant you still had time to try again.

She popped open the frosty bottle and turned it bottoms up. She guzzled as much as she could stand. She wasn't properly drunk yet and she wanted to celebrate, have her own private party. She'd picked up a one-layer cake at the grocery store deli and had them write in big orange letters, HAPPY BIRTHDAY, BARB: 35 AND STILL KICKING. Okay, so she'd lied when they asked how old she was. But she'd gotten away with it. No one said, "You look older than that to me, dear." They'd laughed, the two women in their aprons smudged with various shades of frosting. Then they started making jokes about reaching their sexual prime and congratulated Barb for coming a little closer. The bakers were having such a good time teasing her that she didn't mind the private nature of their conversation. Apparently they'd been talking about sex and primes for most of the afternoon since the short, roundish worker had read an article about 'mature orgasms' in the latest Cosmo.

Humph, some prime. If she and Alfred did it twice a month, she considered herself lucky. Not that it wasn't still pleasant. Alfred had his lovemaking down to a science. Sometimes she caught him glancing at the digital clock by their bedside. If it was close to 11:30, she knew things would soon grind to a halt and if she intended to reach orgasm, she'd better hurry along. Then, right on schedule, she and Alfred would climax at exactly the thirty minute mark. Alfred prided himself on his ability to go for a full half hour.

After it was over, he'd kiss her once, tell her he loved her and they'd both roll over and be asleep within minutes. At least Alfred would soon be snoring. Sometimes it took her forever to settle into sleep.

Barb finished off her drink. She looked at the half-eaten cake (she'd eaten the 35 part off in case there was any left for her family. She didn't want them to know she'd lied) and decided she wanted something more, a different way to celebrate.

"I need music!" She said it aloud and something about talking to herself in the empty house made her feel free. Loose and free. She remembered back to when she was a girl. Oh, how she'd loved Elvis. His dark hair, the front curl hanging in his face, those pouty lips and the snarly way he talked. She could almost hear him saying "Hey, babeh, come on over here to your daddeh." The thought made her shiver.

Barb raced up the stairs feeling like she was barely moving at all. She fell against the banister, but it didn't hurt. A glorious sort of numbness spread through her limbs and she felt light. She was heading for her daughter's room, where she could listen to Elvis on the CD set she'd given Stephanie for Christmas. Stephanie hadn't appreciated the present and used her Santa money to buy CD's from some band called

Eating Pumpkins or Chili Peppers or something. Were they all named after food these days? She was glad Elvis had simply used his real name. No Hollywood showbiz names for him. Just Elvis. It was enough.

She reached her daughter's room and noticed the clothes piled on the floor at the foot of the bed. She sighed. Rather than picking them up the way she usually did, Barb sank down on them and started going through the CD rack against the nearby wall. Elvis was at the very bottom. She turned on the stereo and put the CD in its little drawer.

"Are you lonesome tonight? Are you lonesome tonight?" He crooned to Barb as she leaned back against the foot of the bed. She closed her eyes and listened to the sadness twang through his voice. Yes, she thought to herself. Yes, I'm lonesome. And not just tonight. She felt herself becoming sleepy, so she pressed the button for the next song. She wasn't ready for a heartache just yet.

"Return to Sendah, address unknown, no such numbah, no such zone." Better. Barb started dancing on her knees, then lumbered to her feet. She be-bopped over to Stephanie's dressing table and found a book of matches in the table's secret drawer. She lit a fat white candle and turned off the lights. She continued to move to Elvis' beat, watched her hips sway in the mirror.

"Not bad for an old lady." She talked aloud again, liking the sound of herself. She began to sing along with Elvis in a bold voice. Her pants were a little tight around her waist, what with the cake and wine coolers. She unzipped them and pushed them around her ankles, then stepped out. She kicked them onto the pile at Stephanie's bed. Then, in one smooth movement, she curled herself out of her sweatshirt and danced in front of the mirror in her bra and panties. White cotton on white cotton.

Just the kind her mother had always recommended and the kind she swore she'd never wear. But she'd ended up with them anyway, one of her weapons in the battle against yeast infections. Although she wore the middle-aged uniform of her mother, she didn't look much like her. Of course, her strongest memories were the ones right before her mother died. Her mother never had the jiggles Barb saw on her own body as she wiggled in front of the mirror. No, when her mother hit 44, her body had been beaten to a fine thin line. Chemotherapy, cancer and death danced on her mother's features, each taking its turn with her. Barb remembered how she'd looked after the mastectomy. Not that she'd shown Barb anything. But one morning Barb got up early to fix a special breakfast. She'd taken the tray, complete with flowers, to her mother's bedroom. She'd knocked, but there was no answer. So Barb slipped in through the slightly open door.

Her mother stood naked in front of the mirror. One hand cupped the remaining bosom, the other fingers traced a large, red scar that was in place of her other breast. Barb watched as her mother stood and silent tears dropped from her wet face onto the swollen scar, making it shiny in the morning sun.

Barb quietly backed out of the door, tip-toed downstairs, then stomped up again and pounded on the bedroom door.

"At least you're still here." She looked down at her own chest and lifted her breasts. "Maybe a little saggy, but definitely here." She let them drop. She wondered what kind of bra she could buy that would be sexy, but comfortable. Seemed like all the sexy ones were for the A cups. Barb had never been an A. Her training bra was a C.

"You ain't nothing but a hound dog, crying all the time." Elvis interrupted her thoughts and she started doing the Twist, then switched to the Peppermint Twist. A quick glance in the mirror told her she still had it, that rhythm, that great little wiggle.

She watched herself continue to dance, adding a bump-and-grind here and there. The wine made her dizzy and she felt carefree. Before she had time to consider what she was doing, she stepped out of her cotton briefs and flung her bra in a wild circle. She didn't even care where it landed.

There she was, naked and twisting. By now, Elvis had slowed down to "Teddy Bear" and Barb began to thrust her pelvis in and out, her arms wrapping around an imaginary lover. She let her hands drop to her own waist and followed the curves she found there. A curious finger traced over her pubic hair, soft and delicate as feathers. Then, her hands found their way to her breasts.

"Still too heavy. That's why you sag, you know. If you'd just lose some weight, you'd feel so much lighter. Like balloons." Barb giggled. She thought of herself as one of those balloon animals that clowns could create by bending and blowing and twisting.

Elvis continued crooning and Barb plopped haphazardly on the stool in front of Stephanie's dresser. She picked up some lipstick, a dark red, and painted her lips. Then, on impulse, she drew a circle outlining her aureole, first the right breast, then the left.

"No lumps. I check you every month and so far, so good." Barb placed a large dot of color on each nipple. "You've never been quite in fashion, you know. Remember Twiggy. I tried to bind you up so I'd look just like her but out you'd pop no matter what I did." Barb drew a smiley under first one nipple, then the other. "I should name you. Let's see. How about Lucy and Ethel?" She took a breast in each hand and made them nod up and down.

"You like that, huh?" Barb began moving herself in circles and watched as her neon nipples circumnavigated a tiny scratch in the mirror. She liked the heavy way they moved, leaning one way, then the next.

"So Lucy, you're a little bigger than Ethel. Makes you sag more. But that's okay. And Ethel, I really like the way you point directly in front of me, not at the floor like poor Lucy. She's headed in the wrong direction." Barb slugged down the last of her wine cooler. Elvis was finished with his song so she struggled over to the CD player and removed one disk, then put in the next. While Elvis made his social commentary about life "In the Ghetto", Barb sank into the pile of dirty clothes at the foot of Stephanie's bed. She liked the feel of her skin against the various fabrics, the scratchy wool of a sweater, the rough carpet, a silky nighty, flannel boxers.

The room spun slightly as Barb sat up again. Elvis crooned "Love Me Tender."

"Oh, baby, I love that song!" She swayed to her knees, her arms hugging her torso tightly. She closed her eyes and moved back and forth, singing along with The King.

"Never let me go." Barb's fingertips found her breasts and she circled each one. Then, with a long sigh, she fell back against the pile of clothes, her head filled with Elvis and romance, her painted chest a red smear.

CONFESSIONS OF A FAT WOMAN

April 22, 2001

Dear SlimJim,

Strange name for a diary, especially coming from a woman who weighs close to four hundred pounds, but I like the idea of a skinny "silent partner." That's what my weight-loss counselor, Dr. Dilly, calls you. She says that keeping a record of my progress is as important as exercise and eating the right foods. So, partner, here goes:

I don't know what it's like to jot down ideas, to use words to slice through layers of fat and lay open my heart. Dr. Dilly says it will be therapeutic and I'll come to love you. I hope so. I want to love somebody.

I'll start by writing about you, SlimJim. That's easier than thinking about myself or my husband, Gator.

Your cover is peach-colored around the edges with a big sea shell in the middle. Pale greens and shades of coral swirl inside the conch making it look like some kind of unending riddle. I'm proud to put my thoughts down in such a book, even though the pages aren't lined and my loopy scrawl heads down, then rises back up, spinning like a top trying to straighten itself.

Dr. Dilly, isn't that a funny name? Makes me think of Dilly Bars, ice cream on a stick slathered with chocolate. I hate the thought of giving those up, but Dr. Dilly's so encouraging, sometimes I believe I can leave the "world of sugar and fat," as she calls it. Yep, I want to journey out of that place and hike my way into the land of lean.

She's not a real doctor, though. She told me they'd given her an honorary degree from the little college in West Virginia where she earned her R.N. because she'd made such a success of helping fat people. She even helped the dean of the college shave off fifty pounds. She was assigned to me at the weight loss clinic where my grandfather sends me twice a week in Raeford, North Carolina, about twenty miles west of Dunderach, where we live.

It's tobacco country, and Papaw owns a big chunk of the county, over three thousand acres. We farm some and rent out the rest to the lumber companies. I've been working in tobacco all my life, snapping off the suckers, stringing, nurturing each plant until we carry truckloads of the big old leaves to market. We raise a little tobacco for our own use, along with a large vegetable garden. Every other year, Papaw grows soybeans in the smaller fields out back of the house.

Actually, I don't farm any more, I haven't since I got married three years ago. But for a while, Papaw and I had a real system going.

Dr. Dilly has done some crazy things to help me get started on my program. She made me close my eyes and think back to when I was little. I was supposed to "visualize the fat-promoters of the past." I squeezed my lids tight as I could, but all I could see was fireworks going off. Then I remembered.

I wasn't always fat. My baby pictures showed a normal-sized child with straight blondish hair and a happy smile. In my favorite shot I'm sitting on Mama's lap and her chin's resting on the top of my head. She's a slight woman and doesn't wear any rings on her fingers. But she looks right at the camera, almost defiant. I'm about three years old, and that's the only picture I've got with Mama in it.

The next photo of me is in first grade and I'm already starting to fill out. Mama died before I turned four and I went to Papaw, him being my only relative. I remember waking in the middle of the night, crying. Papaw would stumble into the room, rub the top of my head with his rough hand, and give me a cookie. Sometimes I called for ten or more chocolate chips to settle me back to sleep.

I took to sweets and Papaw took to me. When the other kids made fun of me for being chubby, he'd tell me a smidgen of weight on a woman was a good thing. "If your mama'd had more meat on her bones, she might have lived through the pneumonia." Papaw said he didn't figure to lose another woman. Besides, he needed somebody big and strong to help run the farm. At least that's what he told me. I didn't realize growing up that Papaw could have hired any help he needed, that we were what some people might call rich.

We never lived wealthy, though Papaw's old farmhouse was too big for just the two of us. And Papaw, why he'd kick and fuss if he had to wear anything but his bib overalls. He didn't have any use for people who were "high-falutin'."

So I grew to suit him, tall like my no-account daddy, an equipment salesman who passed through Dunderbach on his way to the coast. He stayed three weeks, long enough to sell Papaw a secondhand cultivator and talk my mama out of her drawers.

My point is that I wasn't always fat. At the start of things, I was a normal size. I gaze at those baby pictures and think about how cute I used to be, one dimple in my chin. Not like now, dimples everywhere.

May 3,

Dear SlimJim,

Dr. Dilly is pleased with my progress. So far, I've lost five pounds. Pretty fast work, she says. She makes me walk everyday, even on the days when I don't go to group sessions. The first week I huffed and puffed my way for one full mile. My heart beat like I was in a parade and my face turned red and pulpy like a Big Boy tomato. But now I'm up to a mile and a half. When you try to move 376, I mean, 371 pounds, that's work. But I hit the trail every day and the thump, thump isn't a bass drum anymore. More like a snare, lighter and more steady.

Dr. Dilly strolls with me on Thursdays and we talk, or rather she talks. I'm breathing so hard I can't get a word out. She tells me about how she lost over 100 pounds fifteen years ago, when she was in her early thirties. Her hair's cut short, bright red with a few gray streaks. She's shorter than I am, and older, but she's still no skinny-minny. Not that she's fat either. She's just right with well-muscled arms and legs.

She said as soon as I lose twenty pounds, we're going to do some exercises in the pool at the Y. When she first mentioned it, I panicked. I wouldn't want anybody to see me in a bathing suit, the white rolls of flab hanging out like lumps of dough. All the people staring.

But she said the two of us would swim for a short time, like a half hour, and we'd be the only ones in the pool. I figured that would be okay. After all, it's her job to look at fat people. She shouldn't be surprised at the rippled skin that's been stretched to its limit.

She told me to keep writing about how things were for me growing up. She said sometimes when you write stuff down, you begin to understand your life better. I don't know about that, but I'll give it a try. She's counting on me.

Papaw used to call me his own bale of cotton and I looked

like one, no shape, no indentation from head to toe. But I didn't care because I was strong and Papaw depended on me, just like he would a son. I was taller than the other girls, 5'8" by ninth grade. And I was broad with shoulders perfect for hoisting tobacco or hay. Most of the boys in junior high challenged me in arm wrestling at least once. Nobody beat me, though, not until Petey Scoggins started weight-lifting his senior year of high school.

By the time I graduated, I weighed close to two hundred pounds. Not one boy'd asked me on a date, and at the church youth group, I always sat with the leader, Mrs. Cotter.

I knew what went on between men and women, though, despite my own lack of firsthand experience. Growing up on a farm you can't help but figure it out.

Papaw never said anything to me about such things. What I learned, I picked up from health class at school, the other girls, and the farm animals. The whole idea scared me, especially when I thought of being locked up with any of the boys at school. Not that I had to worry about that. I could still take most of them in a fair fight.

As things turned out, no one showed the least interest in me and I was glad. That is, none perked up around me until Gator Jones.

May 21,

Dear SlimJim,

Dr. Dilly said I might as well get on with the business about Gator. I'm doing fine on the diet and when she weighed me this week I'd lost all together almost 20 pounds. She said it would come off quick at first since I had so much to lose. Enjoy it while it lasts, she squealed when she read my weight on the scales. She gets more excited than I do.

So far, the diet I'm on hasn't been that hard to follow. But some nights right after the 11:00 news, I get real sad. I think about buttering food: corn, biscuits, toast. And how I probably won't ever again taste the salty, half-melted sweetness on a homemade roll still warm from the oven. I try to limit my thoughts to butter, but sometimes ice cream weasels its way into my brain and I cry a little. Seems like I'm giving up everything good in the world. Which brings me to Gator.

I know I've avoided talking about him. It makes me sad to remember how things were between us. But, I guess Dr. Dilly knows what she's doing, although that exercise where I rubbed myself with petroleum jelly didn't quite work. The vaseline was supposed to help the fat melt away easier, but all it really did was mess up my clothes. I'm dodging Gator again. Well, here goes:

I haven't seen Gator since the days following my heart attack. Imagine, me, twenty-one, having something like that. But, like Papaw said, I was too much of a good thing.

After the heart attack I decided to lose weight, and that's when Gator started acting strange. He'd bring me food, the bad kind like french fries, donuts, anything sweet and gooey.

But I guess I'd better back up and explain about Gator and me. His real name's Gaither, but folks around here call him Gator cause his daddy lived in a little shack near Crawley Swamp. I'll never forget the first words he said to me the summer I graduated.

"You sure are one fine-looking woman. A little too skinny for me, but still fine." It was a hot afternoon in August when I was in the middle of putting up hay for Papaw. There I stood, balanced on the ledge of the loft, hefting a bale into place and Gator yanks my attention away from the job at hand. I almost lost my balance and teetered on the brink of the old pine plank for a second, wobbling like one of those blowup punching bag clowns.

"Shut up. Keep your pea brain on your work." He was supposed to be forking up the hay that had fallen from the bales, sweeping and raking it into a pile. No boy'd ever said anything like that to me before and I figured he was making fun.

"You're even cute when you're mad." He returned to his raking, the steady scrape of the metal prongs against the dirt giving me a rhythm for my work.

You can see why Gator's sweet talk rubbed me the wrong way. A runt like him (he was slim as an Oscar-Mayer weiner) would be just the kind to poke fun at me, a big, ugly girl with a face round as a cantaloupe. I didn't want him at our farm to begin with, but Papaw got it in his mind that we needed help that summer.

"Sissy, you know Gator Jones? Coupla years older'n you, I reckon." Papaw spit a wad every once in a while from his rocker on the front porch. He liked nothing better than a chaw after supper.

"Yeah, I've seen him around." The setting sun was a bright peach, the surrounding sky going red in blotches.

"I hired him to help us out." Another splat hit the dirt.

"Why? I can handle everything. Always do." I couldn't believe he'd take on another worker without talking to me first. We were partners.

"I'm close to seventy, girl. And you. You ought to be thinking about what you're going to do with your life. You're a young lady. Working this farm'll wear you out before you know it." He kept his eyes on the clouds that were moving in fast.

"I've been working like a man on this farm since I can recall. Besides, that Gator's too little to do the kind of work we do. He ain't big as a titmouse." I'd seen him down at the feed store, a small man a head shorter than me, his biceps the size of my ankles. What good he'd serve, I couldn't guess.

"How big's a man got to be to pick tomatoes or feed chickens? I ain't got in mind for him to do much real work." Papaw patted my knee and I knew he still considered me his right hand.

When Gator showed up, his blue jeans baggy as a burlap sack, I didn't take much notice of him. Sometimes I'd catch him staring at me from under the rim of his straw hat when he thought I wasn't looking. His eyes, small and red-rimmed, were pale as the early morning sky, and his skin was speckled with large freckles all the way up his arms. He had scant sideburns he pulled at in his free time and his butt was no bigger than half-risen loaves of bread.

When we'd break for lunch, Gator'd slide into the kitchen kind of sideways like a tom cat.

"Smells good." He said the same thing everyday and for weeks those were the only words I heard him speak after that first day, the day of his compliment.

We sat down to country ham and tomato slices jammed between thick hunks of homemade bread. Iced tea, brewed not instant, and potato salad, sometimes corn on the cob. Gator ate fast and quiet. Me, I liked to enjoy my food so I took small bites and chewed em up good.

Soon as Gator finished, he'd stare at me while I ate. I tried not to eat more than he did, but most days I'd have another half sandwich. His eyes would glaze over and a strange smile settled on his face every time I took a bite. It made me nervous and before long, I made sure I quit eating the same time he did.

One day in late September, he sidled up to me, hands brownish-red from working in the garden, the rim around his fingernails dark and thick with dirt and fertilizer, I guessed from the smell of him.

"I been meaning to ask you something." He faced the setting sun and shaded his eyes with his hand. Even the creases around the corners of his smile were sooty and the sweat beaded across his brow like a bad case of warts.

"Better watch it, or I'll bust you like a hickory nut." He'd got my blood up, staring at me like he was going to poke fun at my square shoulders.

"Take it easy." He seemed sincere and I almost regretted being so mean to him.

"Well, what'd you want?" I kept sweeping off the back porch, little swells of dust bubbling up into the dry air and settling down again to the step below.

"I... I wondered, Sis, if you'd go out with me sometime? Dancing?" A sudden gray cloud blocked the last rays of sunlight, leaving us in shadow. I couldn't see his eyes, didn't know if he was teasing or not.

"Well, I never danced a step in my life." My mouth was dry and I had a hard time speaking.

"I'll teach you. We can practice in the barn after chores. It won't take long to learn." Gator smiled at me and I noticed for the first time that it was a good smile.

"I guess we could give it a try." I turned, leaned the broom against the door frame and walked back inside the house.

That was the start of my serious eating. That strange minute when Gator and I decided to dance.

It's not easy, writing all this down. My stomach is growling hard, like I've done a day's worth of plowing behind a cranky mule. And it's only early afternoon, two more hours until my fruit snack. Thinking about Gator gives me an appetite. When I consider that man, an overwhelming urge for chocolate pound cake hits me. I think I'll take my walk. Dr. Dilly told me to work my legs when I felt weak. And right now, I'm feeble as a newborn mouse.

June 7,

Dear SlimJim,

Today was real hard for some reason. Maybe it was because it was right before my period and I felt the need, the actual need for something sweet. It got so bad that I cried during group. Dr. Dilly held my head in her lap and stroked my hair until I'd used up all my tears. Then we talked about how to handle our hormones, how to make them work for us, not against us. Every other woman in the group told about how she had cravings, just like mine. I didn't feel so bad after that. And I especially liked Dr. Dilly's touching my hair. It stirred something in me, a thing long forgotten, vague as gauze.

June 15,

Dear SlimJim,

I try to make an entry everyday, like Dr. Dilly told me. Usually I get five out of seven, not bad. I noticed after I started writing about Gator, I needed a long pause. In the between time, I realized I write more about food and how hard it is for me to wedge myself in places normal people don't think much about. Like the toilet.

At the farm, we still have an outdoor johnny, like they used to have everywhere. We have an indoor, too. Don't go thinking we're completely uncivilized just because we're country. But I use the one outside cause Papaw made it special for me. It's got an extra wide board to sit on and built-in support. I tried the inside contraption but after I passed 250 pounds I hung all over the sides and it was hard to lower myself onto that little target. In my outhouse, all I have to do is plop down and let go.

And don't forget the front seat of the car. Why do they make those so tiny? By the time Papaw helps me get settled, I've slid over to his side and he has to squinch in. It must be dangerous for him to steer all scrunched up like that.

I hate being slower than everybody else, too. When I struggle into church the ushers share a look of disgust, pure and simple. And I'm in the house of the Lord. I hate to

What You Long For

think how folks who don't know God would act if I should waddle past.

And the pews. Who do you know with a bottom dinky enough to fit one of those hard wooden shelves?

Everything's a struggle and there's no one to blame but me. And Gator.

Gator and I went out dancing, after we'd rehearsed our two-step over and over in the late fall evenings. I worried about finding something to wear since mostly I wore overalls, except on Sundays when I wore what Papaw called my shifts. He ordered them out of a special catalogue and they made me look like a solid wall of daisies. The print was floral every time.

Not that we couldn't have gone to the mall in Raeford and found one of those shops that cater to big women. But I've never been one for shopping. It's hard to enjoy it when you never like the way things look on you. Even dresses that hang pretty on the rack don't look the same when they're stretched and pulled under those fluorescent lights. And Papaw hated to shop in Raeford because the snooty mall clerks'd look at him like he was straight off the turnip truck, even though he could have bought every item in their little shops.

But for my date, Papaw drove me all the way to Raleigh in our '54 rusty-blue truck, and, after a long search, we found a dress to fit. And it didn't have a flower on it.

That night, a cold December Saturday, Gator brought me carnations and a box of candy. I wobbled to his old Ford and tried to let myself into the front seat gracefully. My knees popped, but I don't think he heard them. Besides, I wasn't at my full weight then. I was just beginning.

Later, after the dance was over, Gator drove us to an isolated spot off the main road about two miles from Papaw's house. He cut off the headlights and turned on the radio.

"You hungry?" He turned his face to me and I could see him, a pale ghost in the moonlight.

"Yeah, but nothing's open now. We could go on to Papaw's and I could fix us a couple of sandwiches." Nervous, I twirled the long curl of my big hairdo, the one that hung like a limp piece of licorice at my cheek.

"We got this candy." Something about the way he said it made me blush.

"Okay."

Gator handed me the fancy box and watched, quiet as an apple on a branch. The white ribbon glimmered as I ripped it off. When I lifted the waxy lid, the sweet smell of chocolate filled the front seat. I offered some to Gator.

"You go first," he said with a strange waver in his voice. I didn't see any reason to be shy so I studied the contents of the first layer. The round and square shapes lined up in perfect rows, each piece in its brown crinkled cup. In the milky light, the candy shone like jewels in a treasure chest. Swirls of chocolate formed designs, every one different. Here, a crescent; here a double loop; there, a zigzag like Zoro's signature.

I picked a round piece of dark chocolate and bit the tiniest crumb from its bottom edge.

"Turn on the light so I can see what kind it is," I commanded Gator. He obeyed immediately. The dense creamy center was pink and I could smell strawberries as my teeth sank once again into the nugget, this time all the way to the middle. I felt the sweet flavors melt under my tongue and in the pockets of my cheeks. My mouth filled with a warm syrup and I swallowed. A deep 'Mmmmm' rose out of me. For a minute, all I thought of was the slick feel of the candy sliding down my throat. I forgot all about Gator until I heard him sigh.

I glanced at him. His eyes were all glassy and his face was pink; even in the night air I could see the blood flowing through his cheeks. Every tight little muscle in his body was tense, and he was staring at me the way a hungry cat eyes a mouse. Finally, he noticed I was looking at him and he killed the light in a hurry.

"Don't want to run down my battery. After all, your papaw wants you home by midnight and I don't want problems." His voice was all sugary. He handed the box of candy to me. "Have another one."

At least six hours had passed since my supper and I'd been too nervous to eat much then. Gator and I'd danced the evening through and, I admit, I'd worked up an appetite. I accepted.

Only this time, the minute I cracked into a covered cashew, Gator jumped at the sound and before I knew what was happening, he'd put his hand on my knee. I knew he might expect a kiss at the end of the evening, but this contact was a surprise. I popped the rest of the cashew into my mouth, knowing he couldn't kiss me with my mouth full. I cut him a dirty look. Instead of removing his hand, he started kneading my leg, rubbing the fat around my kneecap between his fingers.

"You got strong muscles here, Sis. Too big for a girl. You ought to be soft all over, soft and cushiony." With his other hand, he picked up a piece of candy wrapped in gold foil. I knew it was the chocolate covered cherry, my very favorite kind. They're always covered in a fancy way.

Gator unwrapped the morsel with one hand and slowly put the whole thing in my mouth at once. I didn't like to eat cherries that way. I'd rather bite a small hole in the chocolate shell, then suck out all the juice, leaving the cherry for last. But what could I do?

I chomped down and felt the sweet juice flow between my teeth. Gator was now rubbing both his hands on my leg, squeezing and poking like I was a lump he was working into something. He didn't hurt me and before I could say anything, he pulled a Coke from under the seat, popped off the lid and handed it to me. It was warm, but after three pieces of candy I needed a sip of something.

I ate the entire pound of candy that night, fed piece by piece with Gator's clumsy fingers, my mouth nicking his knuckles again and again. His hands went over my whole body, rubbing and prodding, his fingers lost, hidden in my secret places. It felt good, not nasty at all, and he never kissed me one time. Once, when his hands were mashing around my thighs, I quivered, a quick spasm in my privates. It lasted no longer than a breath and I think Gator must have noticed and felt something, too, because soon after he grunted and stained the front of his jeans.

We cruised into Papaw's driveway right on time and Gator walked me to the front door.

"I had a good time, Sis. Want to go again next week?" He swept his thumb over my fleshy hand.

"Okay, sure." I stared at the floor, then looked into his eyes which were redder than usual. We shared a secret smile.

In less than six months, Gator and I were married. By then, I'd put on fifty pounds, but he stayed the same. The bigger I got, the better he liked it. He'd bury himself in me, between my breasts, in the rolls of my belly, the folds of flesh under my arms. Anywhere he could get me to wrap around him, he'd put himself there.

Where once I'd been big but sturdy, I became soft like butterscotch pudding. Yielding, is what Gator called it. And he liked the new me, no muscles, just roly-poly. He wouldn't let me lift a finger around the house. No housework, no helping Papaw. I started to feel like a queen bee. The more I weighed, the harder it was to get myself up off the couch. I got no exercise and by summer, Papaw had to hire a couple of workers to help him. By then, Gator had decided to go to the community college to study auto mechanics. He worked days and went to school three nights a week.

He brought me food, ham and eggs for breakfast along with butter biscuits. For supper, mashed potatoes and gravy, meatloaf, macaroni and cheese. Gator spent his spare time searching out new recipes to try. I'd never seen anyone so interested in my appetite.

By the time we celebrated our first wedding anniversary, I'd gained a whole other person. Papaw told me to go see a doctor, said he was worried about me. I obeyed him out of respect but while the doctor rattled off a diet, I thought about Gator kissing me, licking me between the folds of my skin right after he'd bathed me real good.

They just didn't understand, they couldn't know the special way Gator and I felt.

July 13,

Dear SlimJim,

Then came the day of the heart attack and my life looped around like a roller coaster.

Papaw came to the hospital, talked to the doctor and stole me, took me straight home to the farm.

"That Gator's gone kill you. No doubt about it. You're as big as anything I ever saw." The words hurt though he said them kindly. I knew he was worried and I worried right along with him.

Papaw fixed a bed for me downstairs and started me on this Doctor's Weight Loss program. He'd taken me while Gator was at work, but that very night Gator came to whisk me back to our home.

"You can't steal my wife. She belongs at home where I can tend to her." Gator stood in the doorway, his hands resting against the frame. Papaw faced him, his rifle at his side.

"I know what you're up to. Feeding Sis to death. She ain't coming with you." Papaw took a step forward and raised the gun.

"I ain't doing anything but taking care of my wife. Her getting sick's not my fault. I'm good to her, real good." Gator glared at Papaw and they both seemed to have forgotten I was there. Then Gator pointed at me.

"Why don't you ask her who she wants to live with? Ask her, go ahead." I could see Gator's eyes peering in at me, sure as morning that I'd choose him. But I couldn't. That heart attack scared me, my chest caving in like a boulder was pressed on it. And I didn't like doing nothing but eating. I missed working in the soil and running the vacuum. I missed having energy for a movie or to go dancing. Gator hadn't taken me out since we married.

"I aim to stay here for a while, Gator. Just till I get my strength back." My voice was soft, but firm. He didn't say a word as he stalked off the porch.

July 31,

Dear SlimJim,

Gator dropped by again today, plying his wares. Last time it was homemade cinnamon rolls and cherry crisp. Oh God, how good they smelled, all spicy, still warm and yeasty.

Papaw was out in the barn. I don't know how he does it, but Gator times each of his visits to fall when Papaw isn't around. Hoping to carry me off, I guess.

"How you doin today? Been missing me?" He sauntered into the living room where I kept my treadmill. I like to look at it when I'm doing needle work, something I've taken up since I started the program. Dr. Dilly says it's important to have a hobby that can take the place of eating. I've lost close to fifty pounds and I can walk five miles easy.

"Don't sit on that chair, Gator. It's got my needles stuck in it." By this time, I didn't know what to say to Gator. Seeing him unnerved me and so far, each time he'd visited, I'd given in to temptation.

The first time, he took me by surprise with potato rolls and fresh honey. The second time, chocolate raspberry supreme was my downfall. I hated how I felt after eating those forbidden foods, but I couldn't seem to say no to him.

"Doin a pillow?"

"No. It's going to be a picture—The Last Supper. I aim to hang it in the kitchen." I kept my head down, intent on my business. I didn't want to see what he had in his basket.

"Want to take a break? I brought you a little snack—homemade fried pies—apple." He lifted the cover from the basket and the smell of cinnamon and apples filled the room. My stomach growled.

"No thanks. Gator, you know I'm not supposed to eat that stuff. I don't want to gain what I've lost." My mouth said the words, but I could see that special look come into Gator's eyes and I was hungry for more than just food.

"You used to be so good-looking, Sis. Why, you were the finest of all the Jones women. My brothers can't get their women as fat as I got you, honey, and every one of them is jealous. And you're bigger than Ma ever was. I used to be proud of you." His voice cracked the way it did sometimes when we made love.

Gator never talked like that before, never really opened up to me. Ours was more of a secret romance in a lot of ways. I couldn't figure out why he liked me, me being so big and all. I thought he fell in love with me in spite of my size, that somehow, he saw the real me deep inside.

He wasn't in love with the real me at all. All he cared about was how big he could get me. I was some sort of prize heifer like all the boys in 4H used to raise for the county fair.

"You ought to be proud of me now that I'm taking charge of my health. Dr. Dilly sure is." The more I thought about what he'd said, the madder I got. I was nothing to him but a body, a sex object.

"Gator, I don't want you to come around here anymore. Just get on out of here and take your fried pies with you." I didn't raise my eyes and for a minute he sat still. I still didn't look up. I just kept doing my needle work, a stitch in, then pull through. Finally, I heard him step to the door, slam it and jog down the porch steps.

I was weak and trembling. I hopped up, spilling my handiwork onto the floor. My heart was beating fast so I got up on my treadmill and began to walk. The faster I walked, the better I felt. Just like Dr. Dilly said would happen.

Something had come over me, something stronger than the desire to wrap my mouth around a bite of pie. Whatever that something was, I didn't want to lose it. I wanted to be stronger than Gator, stronger than any man. And if that meant going it alone, then so be it. After all, I still had Papaw and I still had the farm.

I remembered how much I used to enjoy thrashing those boys in school, taking down their puny arms with my hard-earned strength. That's how I felt when Gator left with his goodies and slammed the screen door in my face.

At first. But I suddenly missed him, his rubbing and mashing, the way he'd look at me sprawled across our kingsize bed, taking up most of it. I cried then, long and hard.

August 6,

Dear SlimJim,

My muscles are coming back. I can feel little risings on my arms, the backs of my legs. Some days, the desire for food, trays and trays of pie and ice cream, sandwiches with heaps of mayonnaise, makes me think I could eat and never stop, just let my self go again, the way I did with Gator. Surrender to everything. But when that happens, I use the treadmill or go for a real walk around the farm.

I never told Dr. Dilly about the sex, didn't explain how that full-to-busting stomach was the buildup to a relief sweeter than peach cobbler. But I did say Gator was the only boy ever to show an interest in me and he didn't like muscles on a girl.

Now, she's teaching me how to tell when I'm full, something every person ought to know. And she keeps saying she's proud of me. Proud of the weight I've lost, but even happier about the way I've taken to exercise.

I love the way my new body feels moving under the hot sun. I remember how strong I used to be, how Papaw could count on me before my body disappeared into a blob. Now I'm emerging from that cocoon of fat. The woman I'm spinning myself into will be made of muscle pure as gold. I may never be slim as a model, but I'll be healthy and strong, able to work toe to toe with any one. And I'll be the size I want to be, no showpiece, no prize.

WHERE THERE'S SMOKE

This isn't Southern literature. You won't find any farmer-tied-to-the-land theme here; no happy-as-pigs-in-shit redneck families that clutter much of what we call Southern fiction. This story won't be about crazy relatives or racial intricacies. It won't contain any grits or sweet potato pudding. And I promise, there won't be one 'ya'll.'

Instead, you'll discover an urban grittiness; cool, jazzy rhythm and a kind of godless sophistication that will inform the story, which takes place, by the way, in Pittsburgh, that river city, that coal-dusted, steel-blasted city which hangs onto the Appalachians with the tenacity of piglets to their mother's teats. Oops. A farm reference. There'll be no more of those. Change that to the "tenacity of a hooker skimming her favorite corner."

And in this downtown place of graffiti-covered bridges and empty buildings you'll discover Fuego. He's hip, he's ethnic and he's a pervert. Don't worry. He's a good pervert. You'll like him.

You see, Fuego's never acted on his impulses, not once. He didn't even know he had them until his thirteenth birthday when his mother, Isabelle, a woman known for her fierce way with knives, determined to throw a celebration for her only child.

"You a real man, now, my Fuego. We gonna have a party." And she decorated their two-bedroom walk-up with leftover Christmas streamers and a few balloons, the kind he'd never seen before. They were clear and oblong and it didn't take long for him to discover what they'd been intended for before his mother rubbed them against her hair and stuck them on the ceiling. No matter. The effect was festive and soon Isabelle's friends piled into the apartment, sitting on large flowered pillows scattered across the floor. Isabelle turned on the tape player and Peruvian music bounced around the walls of the place. Jo-jo, one of Isabelle's amigos, brought Fuego a cake, one of the day-old jobs they sometimes offered for half-price down at the bakery on 23rd.

Fuego never forgot the one piece of advice his mother gave him that day:

"Keep it in yo pants, little man. Women ain't nothing but trouble," when she'd had enough Tequila to slur over the words of the birthday song. Everybody slapped him on the back and nobody seemed to notice how red his face was at the mention of what was in his pants. Even as they joked about it, he had a boner from the excitement of the day. But then, he had one most of the time it seemed. It couldn't be normal, this constant hard-on. He worried under the sheets at night. Now, here was his mom, making fun. He couldn't figure out how his mother knew about his erections, but he would never forget the shame he felt when all their friends laughed.

Jo-Jo, was there with her lover, Alice. And Bandycoot, the card shark, was playing a line with Bernie, the guy who sang in the shower every Saturday night. He lived above Fuego and his mother, and his singing often drove them to drink a little so they could sleep. Isabelle had the help of her tequila and she didn't care if Fuego sipped some Sangria before he trundled off to bed. As for Fuego, he just drank and thought of Alice's little girl, Lambchop.

Lambchop was only three, but already Fuego could see a hint of the woman she would someday become. He'd been asked to baby-sit a couple of times when Alice and Jo-Jo wanted to hang out at the gay bar on Monongohela Drive. Lambchop had curly red hair and brown eyes so dark you couldn't see the pupils. She looked like one of those aliens Fuego'd seen on STAR TREK, the ones with eyes like the black holes of space.

"Daddy? Daddy? Read me Whose Baby?" Her voice was thick, a hoarse quality that made Fuego's neck shiver. And when she scrambled into his lap with that worn-out book in her tiny hands, he felt something he'd only felt once before.

One time, when his mother'd been crying for what seemed like a whole night, Fuego'd found a soft spot, a weak kind of feeling for her in his chest. He put his arm around her shaking shoulders. All he'd wanted was to make her feel better, ease her tears. But the moment his fingers touched her, she raised up her head and growled at him.

"Get the hell away from me." And Fuego'd run into his room, flung himself onto the mattress on the floor and pounded at it until he tired himself out.

That same desire to touch Lambchop, soothe her with the tips of his fingers, bloomed in Fuego's heart.

Lambchop was warm in his lap as he read to her. She helped him, repeating everything often before he'd had a chance to say it. Fuego noticed as her little body relaxed against him and he could smell the baby sweat of her soft head, something else was happening—another hard-on. The weight of her body felt good, but the sensation scared him. He didn't like the pictures that flashed in his mind. He knew he should stop the heat growing in him. He knew he must be a bad, bad boy.

"That's enough. You want something to eat? You want a cookie?" Fuego lifted her off his lap and stood. He took her small hand and led her to the kitchen. After that night, he didn't baby-sit again. When Alice asked him, he told her he was too old for such work, he was a man and needed a real job.

And now, Fuego was indeed a man of thirty-one years, a man without a wife, without anyone in the world. Isabelle died years ago and Fuego kept his shameful secret by avoiding people. He had no friends, no lovers, no family. Even at the elementary school where he worked, he didn't really know anyone. He was the only janitor in a twenty-room building and his job kept him too busy to chat. Besides, who would he talk to besides a few of the older boys from sixth grade? The teachers were young women for the most part and none had shown him more than the required courtesy. Each wanted him to empty their trash in a certain way: Ms. Barns wanted hers collected twice a day while Miss Petry refused to allow him to take it more often than every two days. And there were always the special requests: Could he arrange the desks in a circle? Would he mind if they had a party and he had more than usual to clean up? He did more than they asked, not because he wanted to please them but because he'd discovered the one way he could keep his life under control was to make the world neat.

Order calmed him. His morning routine, black coffee and a large plain bagel with cream cheese at precisely 7:00 AM, started his day. A five-minute shower, a quick rub of the towel, and he was into his neatly pressed uniform. Promptly at 7:30, he caught the bus from the corner across from his building and rode the twenty minutes through the early jammed traffic to school, arriving at 7:50 exactly. On snow days, he rose an hour earlier and walked to the school. He didn't want to take a chance on the bus being late. He always arrived at the same time, regardless of the weather. Fuego considered this his one gift in life—his uncanny ability to keep a neat schedule, to clean his school by military standards, and to order his one-bedroom apartment meticulously.

By now, you must be thinking that we're dealing with an eccentric character, a transplanted 'Southern' creation. Not so. Fuego is exotic, not eccentric. When they live above the Mason-

Dixon Line, such characters as Fuego are exotic. And dark. Allow me to point out that he has no extended family or religious faith to help him wrestle with his desires. He is alone. And while the South has its share of lost, lonely people, somehow it's easier to bear in a climate where the sun greets you each morning with a soft, warm kiss.

The dead middle of the school year was Fuego's favorite time. The sun hadn't risen completely when he went to school, and by the time he'd finished with his cleaning, the dark had settled across the playground and he could barely make out the shape of the jungle gym. He loved the way the cold shine of the streetlights pooled beneath his feet bathing the gray concrete in a cleaner, truer light. Most of all, he loved watching the children, their little faces red with cold, all bundled up, mittens the size of dried leaves dropping at various places about the school. Fuego considered it his personal responsibility to reunite each glove with its rightful owner. He stored his collection of lost items in a basket in the basement where his "office" was. The office consisted of nothing more than a student-sized desk, a grown-up chair and a wastebasket in the boiler room where Fuego kept check on things. The boiler was noisy and old, prone to break down on the coldest days. Fuego's basket of scarves, hats and mittens added a splash of color to the otherwise dreary place. A few of the older students, sixth-graders usually, would volunteer to fetch Mr. Fuego if their teacher had need. But the little ones were terrified of the orange glow from the furnace and the dark brick walls.

Fuego was always pleased when one of the sixth grade boys would venture into his special place. He'd help the boy play hooky by teaching him craps or gin rummy. But Fuego never kept them too long. He didn't want any problems.

One day while scrubbing behind the toilets in the girl's bathroom, Fuego found the smallest mitten he'd ever seen. The hand that fit inside it couldn't be more than three years old. He carefully explored the inside of the mit with his finger, trying to imagine how it would feel to be that little again. Not only was the garment the tiniest in his collection, it was bright purple, a ripe color that he could almost taste. He held it to the light from the boiler and stared at the intensity of color. Then, without further consideration, he placed it on the top of his basket.

He promptly forgot about it. His workload doubled during January with the constant mopping of floors tracked with snow. One especially grueling morning, after Fuego had shoveled through the ice and snow on the sidewalks and mopped up the slosh the children brought in, he was surprised in the middle of a cigarette break in his office by an itsy-bitsy girl.

"Mr. Fay-go, do you got my lost mitten?" The child peeked around the doorjamb and only a tangled mass of wet, blondish hair over a tiny face could be seen. Fuego immediately crushed his cigarette. He didn't allow even the sixth-grade boys to see him smoke. He smiled at the girl and motioned her to come into the dingy room.

"Maybe I got it, maybe I don't. What color?" Fuego considered the size of the girl and knew he had only one mitten to fit those hands. But he wanted to be sure.

"Purple. Real, real purple." The child walked over to him as he bent to retrieve his basket of clothing. The orange glow of the boiler turned her hair to gold and burnished her cheeks so that she looked like a strange, bug-eyed cherub before him.

"I'm not scared to come down here. The other kids are scared, but I'm not." Her voice gave her away and Fuego again felt warmth gathering at his chest. How like an angel she was.

"Nothing to be afraid of down here. What's your name?" He pretended to search through the items.

"Grace Morgon. I'm four-years old and they let me come to the kindergarten because my brother comes here." She stood beside him and he could feel the heat from her body.

"Is this it, Grace Morgon?" He held the purple mitten down low so she could see it easily.

"You found it, you found it!" She threw her arms around him and he couldn't move. She clung to his legs, hugging him. He expected to feel the usual weight grow in his loins and his hands trembled. But nothing happened.

"Be careful not to lose it again. I might not find it next time." He leaned over to her, his face so close he could smell her milky breath. She was like some forgotten dream, dainty, a creature not from this earth. Her nose reminded him of the small, wild strawberries he used to pluck from the edges of the playground near his childhood apartment. He watched as her eyes grew big from their proximity and then without warning, she kissed him on the chin, a wet little kiss, slightly sticky.

"Thanks Mr. Fay-go." And before he could rise from his crouched position, she'd skipped out of his bare room and he could hear the rhythm of her steps in the hall.

You might wish for a more Southern tale, one that would depict Fuego having a twinge of conscience. You'd have all that guilt from a Baptist upbringing to foment in Fuego's heart. Instead, there is no guilt. Fuego is clear and free in his course of action. He intends to win Grace to himself. He wants her to think of him as her 'special' friend.

He begins by finding out which kindergarten room she's in. He discovers her class is Ms. Hopple's, the new teacher fresh from Fordham with the pierced nostril and the tattoo on her left ankle. Ms. Hopple has a haircut like one of Fuego's mother's old boyfriends and she smells of cigarettes and poor feminine hygiene. Fuego heard her say she's making a statement but he couldn't hear what it was she was trying to say. He made it a point to sweep past Ms. Hopple's room at least three times a day to keep an eye on Grace. He didn't trust Ms. Hopple and he wanted to make certain Grace was treated kindly.

After a week of such persistence, Grace began to wave at Fuego each time he passed. Her tiny hand would brush the air and Fuego would feel his heart clinch. He discovered when she would be on the playground and scheduled his outside duty then. Sometimes he would slip her a piece of Juicy Fruit gum when he shoveled snow past where she was climbing on the jungle gym. She'd go to the top and call his name, then wave when he turned to watch her. Seeing her up so high made him catch his breath and he wanted to clamber up there with her, lean against the top bar and shelter her from the cold wind. Instead, he tipped his hat and continued his duties.

Most nights, he'd collapse on his couch with a beer and some French fries, maybe a hamburger. He'd watch the news and thank his lucky stars he'd always kept within the law. After a brief nap, he'd begin scrubbing his small home: floors, toilets, sinks, the outsides of the cabinets, the molding on floors and ceilings. Each job was done with care and by midnight, Fuego could sleep.

Before he drifted off, he'd allow himself to think of Grace. He'd picture her in his apartment, her little form next to him as they watched TV. He imagined she might like those nice programs like Mr. Rogers or Sesame Street. He thought of them together, viewing cartoons, her head on his knee, his hand stroking her hair. Then, after she'd fallen asleep, he'd carry her to bed and curl his body protectively around hers. He would match her breathing and together they'd dream.

Fuego never felt arousal at the thought of her sitting on his lap the way he'd responded to Lambchop so many years ago. When he thought of Grace, he thought of warmth and her hands, the way she smiled and seemed glad to see him. He sometimes remembered his mother and how once in a while, after she'd had enough tequila, she'd come to him while he pretended sleep and brushed his hair from his forehead. How he'd loved her touch. And the smell of tequila still made him feel tender.

As spring melted the snow and the rivers rose, Fuego began to worry about Grace. He was concerned about where she lived. The flood district? Did her parents take enough care of her? Was she being treated well? Fuego knew how cruel parents could be. And he had no reason to believe Grace's people were better than his own had been. So he decided to check out where she lived, investigate these so-called parents and see whether Grace belonged with them or with him. For a strange kind of plan had taken shape in his brain. He wanted a life with Grace and if her folks weren't treating her right, then he'd rescue her. He wished someone nice had rescued him.

"You know your address, Gracie?" Fuego leaned against his broom and watched as the little girl put her finger to her cheek and thought.

"123 Easter Avenue. I member cause my mommy says the Easter bunny lives somewhere on our street, too." She smiled up at him, her strange dark eyes reflecting no light. Fuego noticed a dust ball nearby and the sight of it made him light-headed.

"Good. I might come over. That okay?" He felt like he wasn't really talking. Instead, the words left his mouth of their own accord.

"Yeah. My mommy's nice. You can see my hamster." With that, she ran over to the classroom door and he watched as she hung her jacket on a peg. He quickly swept up the debris in the hall and washed his hands.

That Saturday, Fuego caught a bus to Grace's house. He had to map out his route. He needed to make two exchanges. He didn't like to switch buses but this time it would be worth it. This time he'd learn whether or not Grace needed a rescue.

Now, if this story were set in the South, you wouldn't be feeling quite so uneasy. In a Southern story, Fuego's name would be Barrett Warren, III. Barrett would be the great-grandson of a former mayor of a small, rural town, oh, say, Kernersville, North Carolina. He'd live in the same house his great-grandfather had built, an enormous, two-story white clapboard with a wrap-around porch. And he would have lived there all his life, so that he knew the neighbors on his street and they knew him. He'd share the place with his invalid mama and nobody would talk much about him though they'd all know he was crazy as hell.

And when Barrett would start one of his lawn-mowing phases, the neighbors would go inside and hide until he was through. A few might peek out from behind the curtains to watch as he mowed every yard on the block, his naked chest covered with a sheen of unnatural sweat, his brow dripping like a faucet. But they'd realize that he was harmless, basically. "Barrett never hurt nobody." "Naw, he ain't got it in him to hurt anyone." "He just got to cut the grass sometimes. And when that urge strikes, well, ain't nothing he can do but get the mower and chop down every blade in sight."

And when it was over, Barrett would head home, his eyes dull from exhaustion, the eerie light that had shone out in the heat of his mowing now extinguished. And he would sleep.

The neighbors would rest easy, knowing that whatever took hold of Barrett every few months had now loosened its grip and he'd be once again nice and polite and a credit to his mama. And so what if he decided to trim his hedges at midnight with a flashlight to guide him. And so what if the hedge looked like some sort of grotesque statue in the light of morning. He was Barrett, their Barrett. They knew his family, they knew his whole life and they loved him. As long as he didn't go too far, as long as he kept things under some sort of control. And if he didn't hold himself in line, why they'd just have to kill him.

Not so with Fuego. He had no one to talk to, no one to allow him expression of his new love for Gracie. All he could do was feel his great need for her and try to grapple with it himself. And so he found her house and he stood outside her door, hid himself in the large bushes that covered the crawlspace. The air was icy with tiny crystals and Fuego's teeth chattered. But still he hunkered down, hoping to catch a glimpse of Gracie, praying her mother would do one wrong thing so Fuego could leap from his hiding place, snatch the child and run, run, run to a safe place.

Now the flakes were falling, big, lacy snow, the kind you want to catch on the tip of your tongue, the kind that's wet and sloppy and just right for sledding. Fuego felt them hit his ears and quickly melt. He saw a light go on and heard the murmur of voices. He thought perhaps Gracie had awakened from a bad dream or maybe she'd coughed and her mother had given her medicine. He thought he heard a low growl from inside, but then it subsided. He hoped there was no dog to give him away.

Fuego trembled in the cold. His feet were numb and yet he didn't want to leave. He wanted to guard Gracie, keep every bad thing away from her.

He could no longer keep himself hidden in the shrubs. He had to look inside, see for himself what kind of life Gracie lived. Slowly, he crept to the big double window at the side of the house. The snow had muffled the edges of the world and all was silent. Fuego finally reached the perfect spot for spying on Gracie. He rose on tiptoes and peered in.

Inside, the room was big but cozy, with a fire burning brightly in a stone fireplace. Bluish light from the television cast shadows against the walls. Fuego could see Gracie standing in the doorway, her mother stretched out on a couch opposite the TV. Gracie rubbed her eyes with her diminutive fists. Fuego watched as her mother rose from the sofa and gathered Gracie into her arms. Gracie froze. Her eyes, dark and fathomless, seemed to stare right at Fuego. No one moved. Then, Gracie's mother turned, looked in the direction of the window, and carried Gracie out of the room. Fuego waited and waited but they didn't return. He thought about going back to his apartment, but something held him. He wanted to join Gracie inside, snuggle with her on the couch.

Suddenly, three police cars zoomed up the street. They were going so fast that Fuego couldn't believe it when they screeched to a stop in front of Gracie's house. He kept very still, almost quit breathing. What were they doing here? Was there trouble inside? Was Gracie all right?

The police, in this case overworked city employees who aren't surprised at anything, bear some resemblance to their Rebel counterparts. It's their job to uphold the law. And no matter how rural the area or how far south you go, evil wears the same face. Law enforcement guys meet that face everyday. And now, they've seen the devil in Fuego. A shame, really. But this is a story without mercy.

Before he could consider anything further, officers scurried toward him. He turned to face them and saw that they held guns. He heard a voice commanding him to drop to the ground. Fuego knew that tone of voice. It said 'You're nothing. You're nothing. You're nothing.' And Fuego didn't want to respond to it. Though it called him by name, he didn't want to answer.

Again, the policeman told him to drop. But Fuego couldn't. He didn't want Gracie to see him arrested. He wouldn't fall here, at her place. He decided to run for it. The officer yelled again for him to stop, said something else, but by now Fuego didn't care. All he could think about was getting away from Gracie's house. He heard a pop no louder than a firecracker. A sharp pain above his kneecap caused him to buckle.

Down he stumbled, his face pushed against the frozen ground, the snow a thin layer, not enough to cushion him. When he lifted his eyes, blue uniforms circled him and one of the officers grabbed his elbow. Fuego tried to straighten his shirt beneath his jacket but he couldn't. The idea of his clothes being rumpled made him twitch a little, just a slight pulsing around his eyebrows. He turned his face away from Gracie's house, buried it into the dirt so she wouldn't recognize him.

Now, really. If this had been a Southern tale, that bullet would have whizzed right through Fuego's mismatched heart.

SOME NAMELESS THING

Marissa hadn't known that her bones would sometimes ache once her children left home. No one told her how her joints would occasionally scrape together, a low scratchy buzz that hummed along the length of her skeleton, up her spine until the throb settled dead center in the back of her head. From there, dull pulses of pain shot all the way through to her eye sockets and the only relief was to lie in a dark room with frozen cucumber slices covering her eyelids, making her look like some kind of alien in stasis.

Which explained why she was in the kitchen chopping a big cucumber at five in the morning. Whack, whack, whack, the knife slammed against the cutting board as Marissa stood in the pre-dawn light, her oversized tee shirt hanging to her knees, her bare feet getting cold from the new Florida tiles she and her husband had put in that summer. Her toenails blared bright red, as if some maniac had sliced off the top of each one and left screaming, blood-tipped stumps.

"Damn," she muttered as a dot of cucumber fell to the floor. She leaned over to pick it up and bumped her head on the corner of the island where she'd been working. The gray light, which had suited her earlier, had hidden the edges of things. Her love of the dark and the fact that she refused to wear her new glasses, now resulted in a small lump above her left ear. A lifetime of good vision hadn't prepared to her jump directly to bifocals at 45. She resented the feel of the frame across her nose and kept forgetting to look down when she was supposed to. Maybe a bump wasn't too high a price to pay for ignoring her need for them.

"Think you could be a little louder?" Her husband, James, peered in, his thick graying hair standing almost straight up. His flannel pj's were faded and wrinkled and he looked disgustingly middle-aged.

"Sorry." She cut the last bit of cucumber and packed the slices, two each, in freezer bags.

"Anything wrong?" His voice held that oh-God-you're-a-pain-in-the-ass-but-I'll-try-to-be-kind tone that often set her on edge, but didn't now.

"Can't sleep. Damn headache." She placed the bags in the freezer section of the refrigerator, grabbed a packet filled with ice crystals and hard, green slices of cucumber. She emptied them into her hand and balanced them on her eyes, tilting her head up until it was almost parallel with the ceiling. She tried walking to the bedroom, but soon had to hold the frozen vegetables with her hands. James followed her.

"Don't know why that helps when that stuff the doctor gave you doesn't," he mumbled. She could hear the barely controlled anger in his voice and she almost snapped back at him, but decided it wasn't worth the trouble. She'd learned in therapy to choose her battles. Besides, anger would make her head pound even more.

Marissa eased into their new king-sized, motorized bed (with dual remote controls, no less) enjoying the space it allowed her. She was no longer at the mercy of James' nightmares or his twitching legs. She could lie on her back and spread out like a sunburst. There were no sags anywhere on the new mattress and she loved the way it made her feel—as if she were floating. She placed the cucumber slices on her eyelids and snuggled deeper into the covers. She raised first one hand, then the other and moved them together, now apart, her fingers trailing up one arm, her palms meeting in a prayerlike moment, then reversing themselves. This was her sleep ritual, practiced nightly after James had begun his steady, bass rumble. His snoring had never bothered her. It meant a moment of privacy in the dark, a time she could use to watch her solid hands and arms become translucent, ephemeral, collections of molecules that clung together and seemed material, but she could see the spaces between the atoms, the light that emanated from her. Once she recognized the aura, she began her hand-dance.

Sometimes the slow, sensual movements of her arms became erotic, but usually she simply enjoyed the flow of energy between her fingers. She pulled one palm from the other slowly, then curved her fingers as if she were holding a small ball between her hands. After building the Chi, as she'd learned to call it in Kung Fu class years ago, she often gave the energy to her husband as he slept. She hoped by sharing this, he might be happier, healthier. Then she would build another circle of energy and splash it on her face. It felt warm against her cheeks.

Soon Marissa found relief from her aching head and she drifted in that in-between land of not-quite-asleep-yet-not-awake. It was here she met her children, all three of them.

Downy-headed baby boys. Jack, with golden fuzz barely visible, squirming at her side. Next to him, Mark, first-born, little brown glints of hair, thumb stuck in mouth, fingers splayed across his face, sleeping and sucking, tucked under her arm. And Allen, last-born, dark eyes, dark hair, chubby cheeks still blue and bruised from birth, his hungry mouth searching for her.

She could feel them near her, hear their noises, smell their sweet milk-breath. She remembered showering with them, holding their wiggly bodies under the warm spray of water, mother and baby slippery with Ivory soap. She loved the feel of them against her, their nakedness on her own. Then, toweling off, big baby eyes staring into her face, following her every move. How they had needed her. And she'd been at their command, ready to battle to the death for their safety.

Ringed with their hungers, their needs. Allen's calm gentle spirit, Mark's adventuring soul, Jack's musical, magical heart. She'd been theirs completely. Nothing else in the world mattered, not even James. And she always knew where she was, who she was. She'd answered their calls and it had been simple— keep them safe, keep them safe.

But she hadn't been able to manage it; they weren't safe, not really. The two older boys had made it through college without too much worry. Mark was newly married, Jack in graduate school and living with a woman Marissa barely knew. She realized she couldn't keep them from life, that even in the calmest waters lurked danger. But she didn't carry the burden of their safety on her shoulders any longer. They were, after all, grown men.

Allen was different. He was barely nineteen, headed nowhere. He was her baby and he had broken her heart.

The ring of the phone made her jump and the cucumber slices fell onto her pillow. She knew the call would be from Allen, knew it the way she'd sensed he was in trouble in high school, a certainty coming from the pit of herself. She reached for the receiver in the dark and mumbled a quick, soft 'hello?'

The automatic operator led her through the hoops of reverse-charge calls and finally she heard Allen's voice.

"You in bed, Mom?"

"Just barely."

"I figured Dad'd be awake by now. Sorry."

"No, it's okay, hon. What's up?" She struggled to a sitting position, her head only slightly better, and felt around for the cucumber chips.

"Well... I was... I wondered how you'd feel if I came home for a while." His voice sounded scratchy over the line and she wondered if he had caught a cold. He was living in the mountains and the weather would have turned with the leaves. She knew he hadn't taken a heavy coat with him.

His question twirled in the air like a dead man on a rope.

"Why?" Marissa whispered, not wanting James to hear the concern in her voice.

"I hate it here, Mom. I want to come home."

She could hear his frustration. It ran through his voice like a twisted thread. Her stomach balled up and the pounding in her head resumed with a new fierceness.

"I thought you liked it. Last time we talked, things seemed okay." She tried to keep her voice steady, flat and soft, the way her therapist always spoke. She didn't want to give away any secrets, couldn't stand for him to hear her disappointment.

"I'm lonely. I just feel, I don't know, bad. I don't have any friends. My room is so cold—those maniacs still haven't fixed the heat. I just want to come home."

He sounded so pathetic that she almost said yes. She almost broke her agreement with James, with the therapist. She wanted to tell him to hurry, get the next bus, come home, please come home. Instead, she sighed, a loud, deep breath that shook her achy bones.

"It wouldn't be for long. Just until I can get a job and save up for an apartment."

"I don't know, Al. I'll have to discuss this with your dad. Why don't you call me later?"

"Okay. Sure. Bye."

"Bye, son. I love you."

The click of the phone sounded louder than she remembered. Gently, she hooked the receiver into its cradle and lay back against the pillow. She tried to steady her breathing but it was no use. Everything inside her was beating fast, flowing, twitching. She couldn't stop the quick gulp of a sob that came against her will.

"What's he doing?" James' voice was soft, sad.

"He wants to come home."

"Shit."

"That's what I say. He sounded miserable."

"We knew this was going to happen. I'm surprised it didn't come sooner." He rolled across the extra-wide bed crumpling the sheets and mussing up the covers as he came to her.

"It's okay. We'll talk about it. Don't worry, it'll be okay." His voice wrapped around her like an old quilt.

Marissa felt his arms reaching for her and she moved toward him. She needed those arms now, needed to know she and James were in this together. Tears seeped from beneath her closed eyes and ran down to her chin. They came effortlessly, no sobbing except that first little gulp. She couldn't stop them. Her body leaked out its sorrow and she didn't even feel much, just the warm wetness growing between her face and James' chest.

"I can't bear it. I just can't." Marissa shaped the words with what felt like numb lips. James said nothing.

Her whole body felt as if someone were breaking her, reaching inside and snapping her bones in two, forcing wedges into her joints, pounding and pounding in the deepest parts of her head. Yet she lay still, barely breathing, the steady stream coming from her eyes, warm like blood.

He wasn't a bad boy. On the contrary, Allen was her delight in many ways. Though they'd had to nudge him, well, evict him from the nest, she'd hoped that he might actually fly on the first try. Looking into his mild brown eyes and telling him it was time for him to move away had been the hardest thing she'd ever done. And it had been tough on everyone. He deserved to spread his wings and soar. They all deserved it.

He'd taken their decision well, agreed that things couldn't go on as they had. He even tried to joke a little.

It had been settled, all solved in therapy. And she knew in her heart that he had to help himself now. His life was out of her hands.

Mostly, she'd adjusted very well to the quiet house, the peace that met her at the door when she dragged in from work. She was an assistant librarian, a job she chose for its solitude and silence. During the years her boys were growing up, it meant eight hours of order, eight hours lost among the stacks leafing through any book that caught her eye. Her job had been a reprieve from the chaos at home.

Now she relished the new feeling of discovery she sometimes sensed with James. As if they could relocate each other after all the years. She looked forward to vacation time. They'd talked of travel, a biking tour of France.

Yet, another part of her ached for her children. She found herself on the phone, long distance even in the prime business hours of the day. She needed to hear her sons' voices, check in, make sure they were all right, much the way she'd peeked in on them when they were little.

Allen, especially, needed her now. He was still her baby, her boy. How could she turn him away?

She felt James' hand stroking her head, rubbing the tender place behind her ear.

Slowly, she felt her body go limp, her muscles relax into the slow circles he made around her scalp. Her eyes grew heavy, the lids burdensome. She noticed the regular steady rhythm of James's breath, the warmth of him.

After what seemed like a long time, she gave way to sleep, her body moving away from pain and heading toward something else, something she couldn't name. She knew she couldn't solve this, not here, not now. Yet even without a solution, sleep came, one slow breath after another, the pounding in her head steady as a drum. That she *could* sleep, registered somewhere on her heart. She thought it might mean something, but before she could consider what, she was lost to the pull of the night, the strange peace that came from being at the end of a thing.

THE PERFECT PAIR

Sara Jane Clodfelter and I celebrated every occasion at the Rainbow Café in downtown Winston-Salem—Sara Jane's marriage to George, my first divorce, the birth of Sara Jane's last baby, my second divorce, Sara Jane's resignation from her teaching position after ten long years, my appointment as chief loan officer at the Wachovia Bank. It was here, nestled in our favorite corner table, that I confessed to Sara Jane I was in debt way over my head and she helped me work out a plan toward solvency. It was also here that Sara Jane admitted her many temptations to stray from her marriage. We meditated amid the Rainbow's potted plants and lit candles when she finally decided to turn away from every man but George, laughing that it only took Sara Jane seventeen years to accept monogamy in her heart.

In the early years, we could afford to meet here only a few times, the most special moments, but these days we got together once a week, usually for the Wednesday buffet. I was surprised when Sara Jane called to set up a second lunch date for the week, and she wouldn't tell me why. She said it was a secret and nothing I could do would make her talk. Sara Jane always did love a game. I knew her well enough to know she got a real kick thinking that I'd spend the entire night wondering what she had to tell me.

Now, she studied the menu across from me as if she might order something besides her usual salad. Two business men, one with rimless glasses and a receding hairline, the other with a full head of dark gray hair and a large moustache, scooted into the booth near us. Both were attractive and I saw Sara Jane checking them out. We looked at each other and smiled. At one time, the men might have noticed us, grinned, started a conversation. But now they just mumbled to each other. Sara Jane kept staring at me in a funny way, her mouth puckered as if she'd eaten something sour.

"They've been approved," she whispered.

I knew, given enough time, Sara Jane would make sense. I sipped my ice water, careful to keep the wedge of lemon away from my lips. The rind always left a bitter film in my mouth, drawing my features into a grimace that reminded me of the wicked witch in the Snow White movie. Yes, I was the age now to be an evil step-mother. Sara Jane and I both were. And really, what was so bad about the old witch anyway? She marries a man with a child—a spoiled 'only,' no doubt; she has to adjust to being a mother, teach the girl a proper work ethic, then her husband dies leaving her a middle-aged widow—no wonder the poor woman's insecure, a little hung up about her looks. No wonder she becomes a prisoner of that nasty old mirror.

"I *said* they've been approved."

Sara Jane jolted me, her voice louder than before.

I stared at her, realized I'd been lost in thought. I knew she was dying for me to beg for an explanation. She sighed heavily.

"What's been approved?"

She cut her grilled chicken salad into tiny bites. We'd learned, after years of weight-watching, to make a nothing-meal go a long way.

"My breasts," Sara Jane said. I sensed a sudden drop in conversation between the men in the booth next to us. I stole a glance and caught the guy with glasses with his mouth open, turning away. The other man looked as if he'd swallowed something tasty. They recovered their composure quickly, then each took a bite of bread.

"Not so loud. What in the world are you talking about?" Sara Jane didn't know the meaning of the word decorum. Never had. We'd been in every kind of adventure together over the years and she'd grown even less inhibited as our children left home. She was nothing like me. I was so shy I blushed if Sara Jane said the "f-word." Maybe that was why I hung out with her.

"I got them approved—you know, for a reduction." She smiled and something about the way her eyebrows raised up made me begin to worry.

"You didn't!" I said.

She nodded her head, a dopey-looking grin plastered across her face.

"Why do you want to get a reduction? You're fine. You could give me some—like a transfusion or something." I'd always been small, but I liked my breasts. I really didn't want anything bigger. I was just trying to make her feel better about her own. Not that hers were unattractive—they'd been quite nice ten years ago but she'd put on about twenty pounds since then and most of it seemed to go right to her chest. I knew she had to wear a cast-iron bra to keep them from sagging, but I had no idea she was considering surgery.

"I'm just sick of em. You know, when I was young they were okay. I mean, they got a lot of attention. Like in conversations, you know how men talk to your chest, well, yeah, been there, done that." She took a bite of chicken and rolled her eyes at me.

"Even *I've* suffered eye-to-boob contact." We giggled a little and I noticed again how quiet the two men were in the booth next to us. The guy with the glasses mopped up a water spill while the other man just stared down at the table.

"Well, no more. I'm tired of that. I want to feel light, free. I want them to be perky." Sara Jane's eyes took on a dreamy look and I could see the girl in her, the one I'd known all those years ago.

"Perky is good. Mine aren't exactly perky anymore, either."

"There's the beauty of it—my insurance will pay for this whole thing. See, I got measured and everything. They took pictures, even. So I can get perky and smaller. I think it'll give me a new lease on life. They say you never have to wear a bra again—in your whole life. And they'll never sag." Sara Jane wiped her mouth with the corner of her napkin. She was a pretty woman, though like me, her beauty was fading. Her big brown eyes had always been her best feature but now the lids hung a little heavy and made her look tired.

"Imagine that—never. Sounds good to me." We'd always encouraged each other. When I went back to graduate school, Sara Jane egged me on even though my second husband hated my being in class two nights a week. And when Sara Jane decided to take oboe lessons, I went to her recital and watched as she played that thing like she was born to it.

"So you approve?" She cocked her head to one side and raised her eyebrow again. That sense of worry nagged at me, but I pushed it away.

"Absolutely."

The men next to us were having the world's quietest lunch. I began to wonder if they were mutes.

"Good. Because I need your help." Sara Jane pushed her salad plate away to the middle of the table and lay her crumpled napkin on it, right in the middle of the low-cal dressing.

"Whatever you need, babes, you know you can count on me." I wanted her to depend on me, wanted to be the friend who would help her through this. She'd done so much for me—loaned me her car for a year, listened to me rant about my boring job, showed me how to prepare a perfect pot roast—it was time for me to support her, even when I wasn't sure how I felt about her altering herself like that.

"George's going to take some time off work, that first week at least." That was the first time Sara Jane had mentioned her husband. Their marriage was one of those up/down relationships where she either loved him or hated him. Sometimes, her feelings were hormonally related and sometimes Sara Jane just fluctuated all by herself. I wasn't surprised that George had agreed to the surgery—he'd always given Sara Jane exactly what she wanted. He simply adored her, the same way I did. The same way everybody did.

"So, what do you need me for?"

"You've got to help me find the perfect pair."

"What?"

"Well, I looked it up on the net and this one girl found a perfect pair, the exact kind she wanted. She took a bunch of pictures from all kinds of angles so the doctor would know what she had in mind. She got exactly the kind of breasts she'd picked out. She put them on the net to prove it. I figured that was a good plan." She leaned in toward me. I noticed the men in the booth had finished with their meal but were making no moves to leave. I leaned toward Sara Jane and whispered.

"How in the world are we going to do this, Sara Jane? You just can't go around asking women to photograph their boobs!" I knew I should have listened to my inner voice, the one I'd recently discovered at Yoga class. The air in the booth next to us was electric. The men were actually tilting their heads toward Sara Jane.

"I've got it all figured out," Sara Jane hissed to me.

"Why can't you just look in a magazine? Or on the net? They've got all the boobs you could want." I usually tried

156   Anne Clinard Barnhill

to go along with Sara Jane but this latest scheme sounded a little too nuts for me. After all, I was single again and my only support came from the bank. I couldn't take too many chances.

"I can't go with two-dimensional. Breasts are so much more than that—they have depth and heft, texture and besides, those pictures aren't real. They use glue, you know." She placed her fork across her plate and stared at me knowingly.

"Glue? What do you mean?" I stole another glance at the man with glasses as he just sat in the booth with his friend, both immobile.

"You know, sex glue. Women don't really look the way those magazines have them posed. They do it with glue. Like they glue the breasts up if they're saggy or to one side if they're too little to move on their own." Sara Jane motioned for the waitress and asked for a look at the desserts. She frequently did this, though she never ordered any.

"How do you know this?"

"It's common knowledge. Honestly, Em, you're so naïve. So, obviously I can't make do with pictures. I need the real thing. Don't worry, we'll find them. I have a plan." Sara Jane gave me her most playful smile, more of a grin really. She wrinkled her nose and her whole body seemed to squench up like some sort of deranged elf. Her eyebrow shot up so far it made my legs tremble.

"I've been dreaming about them, you know," Sara Jane said. We were at the Mall, scoping out the young girls, looking for the perkiest, sexiest breasts we could find. What a way to spend a Saturday.

Sara Jane rested her head on her hands like school girl.

"What?" I said.

"Breasts, of course. In my dreams, they're light and fluffy—like little dollops of meringue. My nipples are pointed up to the sky and before I know it, they've lifted me

What You Long For   157

off the ground and I'm flying. I circle around and around my neighborhood, looking down at the children in their yards." She stared at me, her big eyes even bigger than usual. I thought she was going to cry for a moment.

"Oh, my God! Look! No, don't look! We don't want her to know we're watching." Sara Jane grabbed my arm and squeezed.

"Where is she? What does she look like?" I kept my head straight, fearing to turn around, afraid Sara Jane might pinch the blood out of my arm.

"She's in line at the Chinese food place. She's got long red hair. And she's got the cutest, perkiest little boobs I've ever seen." Sara Jane's eyebrows were really arching now and I could tell there'd be no stopping her. Suddenly, everyone at the mall seemed normal and Sara Jane appeared a little over the edge. I wondered for a just a second what I was doing here, with this woman, when I could have been at home puttering in the garden.

"You can look now." She released my arm and I slowly turned to check out the object of Sara Jane's affections. The girl was beautiful, maybe sixteen, with pale freckled skin and waves of thick, rich hair the color of my mother's cherry dining room table. She was tall and thin with absolutely perfect breasts. They were high and round, the kind of breasts artists like to draw for the pure joy of it. No wonder she caught Sara Jane's attention.

"What are you going to do? I mean, you can't just go up to her and say, 'Hello dear, I was wondering if you'd mind if I took a few pictures of your breasts, they're just so lovely.'" I suddenly realized how bizarre the girl might find us, two middle-aged women in sweat pants asking for such a thing.

Sara Jane was out of her chair and on her way to Lin's Kitchen before the words had left my mouth. I grabbed my purse and followed her. I knew I'd have to stop her before she did something she might regret. I should have known better.

"Excuse me, dear, my friend and I were just admiring your—"

"Purse. My daughter's been wanting one just like that. Do you mind if I ask where you got it?" I could barely sputter the words I was so out of breath from keeping up with Sara Jane.

"Oh thanks. I got it at the Gap." The girl ordered two eggrolls and a root beer. Oh, for a young stomach. I took Sara Jane by the elbow and tried to steer her away from the girl, but she didn't budge.

"Do you go to school around here?" Sara Jane smiled at the girl, then continued. "I have a son at Grimsley."

"I go to East. But sometimes we play Grimsley in football. They usually win." The girl paid for her food and looked like she wasn't quite sure what to do next. I could tell she wanted to go eat her food, but she didn't want to be rude to what she probably thought of as two old ladies.

"What year are you?" Sara Jane followed the girl as she approached a nearby table.

"Junior."

"Oh, I remember my junior year—the prom, all those algebra tests." Sara Jane sat down right across from the girl while I stood beside her. "Do you mind if we join you?" What could the poor kid say? She was too polite to tell us to beat it. I sagged into the chair next to Sara Jane.

"What's your name?"

"Allison."

"What a pretty name. My name's Sara Jane. I always hated that name. So plain. Old-fashioned. And this is my friend, Emmie." I smiled, tried to let the girl know we were harmless.

By the time Allison had finished her lunch, Sara Jane had told her all about her son, about how she was now teaching oboe lessons and about her upcoming surgery. She went into great detail about the procedure and Allison began to look a little pale. Then Sara Jane explained why she needed Allison's help.

"I can't imagine what's taking her so long," Sara Jane said as she took a bite of frozen yogurt. We'd had quite a conversation with Allison and Sara Jane treated us to the yogurt. (She said Allison deserved it.) But then Allison had to go to the bathroom. That was at least twenty minutes ago.

"She's ditched us. I don't blame her," I said.

"We'll give her five more minutes. Then we'll find somebody else," said Sara Jane.

I must say the girl took everything well. She nodded as Sara Jane told her why she wanted to take pictures of her breasts and didn't seem to think we were crazy. She practically 'yes-ma'm'd' us to death. But now, she'd escaped.

I noticed a man in a brown uniform scanning the food court. He wore a badge.

"There's a policeman over there. You don't think Allison reported us, do you?"

"Of course not. Why should she? But I am getting a little worried about her." Sara Jane scraped the bottom of her cup and slurped up the last bit of yogurt. I watched as the officer headed in our direction.

"Excuse me, ladies. Would you mind coming with me to the mall office?" The young man couldn't have been thirty. His taut skin was clean-shaven and he had no lines anywhere. He reminded me a little of the Gerber baby all grown up, that's how sweet he looked.

"We certainly do mind. Why do you want us to go to the office?" Sara Jane's tone was high-handed, as if she were the boy's mother. Well, she could have been. We both could have been.

"I'd rather not say here, ma'am. It's a private matter." The officer tried to look at us in a stern, no-nonsense way. I could tell this wasn't easy for him.

"Well, young man, you'd better say. I'm not in the habit of going off with men, even if they *are* wearing a uniform." Sara Jane smiled up at him, her eyebrows raised up. I knew she was doing it to make her eyes less droopy. She was using her old standby, her charm. I didn't think it would work. The boy was too young.

"Ma'am, there's been a complaint…" He lowered his voice and a blush crept up his neck to his face.

"What sort of complaint?" Sara Jane straightened in her chair. She bent toward the name tag on the officer's shirt. I knew she couldn't read it without her glasses but she'd never put them on now—Sara Jane considered reading glasses a sign of weakness, a sign that age had, indeed, placed his hand on her shoulder. "Officer… officer Tim Goiter."

"That's Jim Corder, ma'am. The complaint was made by a young woman. As I said, it's of a personal nature and I'd rather discuss it in private. So, if you'll come with me…" the young man sounded very persuasive, almost kind.

"Let's just go with him. We don't want any trouble." I didn't want a scene and I knew she was more than capable of starting one. She'd been a hippie back in the 60's and demonstrated for everything from civil rights to the rights of chickens to be free-range. She stared at me when I said it, as if I were the lowest person on the planet.

"He's not the MAN, Em. He's a mall cop, that's all."

I kneed her under the table, and tried to remind her of my new promotion at the bank. Bankers don't like it when their employees are in the newspapers. They want their employees to blend, blur into the crowd of successful, competent and trustworthy business people that run the world.

"Okay, okay. We'll come peacefully, Officer—."

"That's Corder, ma'am."

The interior of the mall office was beige. I mean, entirely beige. The walls, the carpet, the file cabinets, the curtains,

What You Long For 161

the plastic furniture, even the fake paintings on the wall. Officer Corder stood in stark contrast in his deep brown uniform. A forest brown, the color of tree trunks.

He sat behind the desk and indicated that Sara Jane and I were to take the two seats in front of him. He pulled a form from a file and began to fill it out. We watched in silence.

"What's that?" Sara Jane finally asked, her voice ripping the stuffy silence of the room.

"Just some paperwork. Every time I get a complaint, I'm required to fill out one of these." I could see the young man's flushed face and neck. In the small room, the shade had deepened.

"Well, you can't just hold us here while you piddle around with that form. What are you charging us with?" Sara Jane's voice seemed shrill and I noticed that she, too, was had turned red in the face.

"Ma'am, a young girl accused you of trying to talk her into taking nude pictures. Now I know that's really an unlikely story. You two ladies look like nice women. But I'm required to check into every complaint…" Officer Corder was obviously uncomfortable accusing women his mother's age of sex crimes.

"We didn't want naked pictures—only her breasts." Sara Jane gave me a look that said "what a conceited little strumpet to think we wanted her entire body!"

Office Corder blanched and I was glad he was already sitting down.

"You mean, you actually *did* proposition her?" At that, Sara Jane stood up. She wasn't an imposing person physically, about 5'3 at most. But she could scare the wits out of grown men twice her size—I'd seen her do it with George and their three sons. There was something about her voice and her fearlessness than just wilted them.

"Young man, your mind is in the gutter. Now, I'm going to explain this one time and one time only. But first, I'm going to open that door. It's hot as blazes in here." Sara Jane marched over to the outer door and yanked it open. She stood there for a moment fanning herself. Oh no, I thought, hot flash. I knew Officer Corder was in for it now. We might not get out of this without jail time after all.

"You have no idea what perimenopause is like, do you? Of course not. You can't imagine what it's like for your body to rebel against its natural clockwork, to suddenly stop what it's been doing for thirty years. No, I don't think you can." Sara Jane walked around behind the desk until she was towering over Officer Corder. He looked up at her, his features blank and amazed.

"Well, let me tell you, it's Death. I mean it's Death slapping you right in the face. You can no longer believe you'll live forever. That's out the door, mister. And you can't fool yourself about looking young, either. Another hope squashed under the heel of time." Sara Jane pointed her finger in the young man's face. Her own was beet red and her eyes seemed to be going in different directions all at once. I knew she'd been having trouble. Her periods had become irregular and strange just as mine had. We both wanted to fight against age, but how? Sometimes it felt like all we did was battle—against men, against the cult of youth in our society, against the idea that now we were superfluous, now we could be discarded like worn-out tennis shoes because our child-bearing years were gone. Sara Jane rattled on, her voice rising, straining against the air in the small room.

"You men, you don't have such a slap in the face. You get to pretend for years that life has no consequences, no end in sight. But for us, it's different. And it's sad, mister. It hurts. All I wanted was a picture of her boobs to show my plastic surgeon. That's all. Is that crime? Is it? Is wanting perky, new breasts a fucking federal offense?"

"Sara Jane, settle down. You're going to have a stroke if you don't relax. Sit down. It's okay." I led her to her chair and helped her collapse into it. She was panting, but the tension was holding in her shoulders. She refused to droop.

Sweat streamed down her face. Her color had gone from red to pale white and I knew the flash was over. I also knew Officer Corder was going to let us go.

"Ma'am, I'm sorry. I didn't mean to cause you trouble. I'm not even going to fill this out. You're not banned from the mall or anything." The young man stood next to his desk and looked confused. I stood over Sara Jane, talking to her softly, patting her shoulders. Finally, she stood up. The young man, looking very relieved, took Sara Jane by the elbow and escorted her out of the office. I followed behind them. I was touched by his kindness, his willingness to understand a little.

"Thank you, officer. I can take care of her from here." I gave his arm a gentle squeeze and linked my arm through Sara Jane's as we slowly strolled from the office into the mall.

"You want some coffee? Decaf. Definitely decaf." I patted her.

"Sure, why not?"

We found a quiet restaurant at the entrance of the mall and it was dark inside. A young waitress showed us our booth and we could see the mall fountain and all the people as they headed for the stores. Most were young, mothers with babies, teen-agers, entire soccer teams still in uniform. Sara Jane was silent while I ordered our coffee. I, too, kept my thoughts to myself as I watched the people outside. I don't know how long the two of us sat like that, not talking, just observing. A sort of peace settled on us, like a long sigh of relief, the kind that comes at the end of the day, the kind that is ready to accept the gifts of the night.

Suddenly, Sara Jane sat bolt upright in her seat.

"Don't look now," she sputtered.

"What?" I sipped from my cup.

"That girl over by the fountain. She's got the most perfect set I've ever seen. And she seems older than little Allison—more mature." Sara Jane's eyebrows raised just a little. I felt nervous, but surely, after what we'd just been through, Sara Jane would know better. Surely, she'd had enough for one day.

"We could just go meet her, get to know her. You know, we went too fast with the last girl. We need to take our time." She took hold of her purse as if she were going somewhere. "It'll be different now."

"Sara Jane—don't. Let's think about this. I may have an idea." I didn't have an idea at all, but I wasn't ready for another ordeal.

"What? What's your idea?"

"Let's go to my house and I'll tell you." I didn't know if she'd be put off or not. *She* was the one who could hold secrets, not me. But I had to try.

"Okay. I'm sick of this mall air anyway." Sara Jane and I walked from the restaurant and I said a little prayer for inspiration on the drive home.

"Want some wine? It's a little early, I guess, but what the heck." I turned on the ceiling fan in the kitchen and opened up the fridge. Sometimes wine brought on a hot flash so I always took mine over ice with the fan going full blast. Even in winter.

"Why not?" Sara Jane plopped on the bar stool and watched me pour the wine into the fancy glasses I usually kept for company. I knew she'd be impressed that I took such care with her today.

"So, what's the plan?" She came straight to it as I knew she would. I still didn't have a plan.

"Now let me understand—you want to actually see the "breasts, right?"

"Yeah." Her face became serious and she explained, "The doctor wants me to go to a size C. I was thinking along the lines of a B, but who knows? I'm a damn double D, so how am I supposed to know the difference between a C and

B? It's like alphabet soup." She ran her finger around the rim of the glass, then licked the tip.

"I tried to guess which size I wanted by looking at bras in WalMart but it's so hard to judge. I poked my fist into the cups but people kept looking at me funny. Besides, fists aren't shaped right." Sara Jane took another big sip of the wine and it left a little stain across her lip.

"It *is* a big decision. I mean, I guess it's something you'll have to live with the rest of your life." I, too, gulped the wine more quickly than usual.

"Damn straight. And that's why they have to be perfect." She paused and looked at me for a long moment. "Am I crazy, Em?"

"I don't think so. I'm thinking about a face lift myself at some point. Maybe." I *had* been considering it but I'd never said the words before. Who could *not* consider it in this day and age? After all, I still had my career but younger people nipped at my heels already. It seemed nothing more than a wise business investment to look as young as possible.

Suddenly, a plan formed in my mind and before I could think about it, the words sputtered out of my mouth.

"You want to see mine? I'm a B. It might give you an idea." I'd never showed my breasts to a woman before, never even thought about it. All those years of friendship with Sara Jane, we kept our bodies to ourselves. We held on to our modesty, like most women, I imagine. I don't know what made me so ready to show myself to Sara Jane now, except that I loved her and she needed my help. I didn't want to see her get arrested and I wasn't sure I could trust her not to do something rash on her own.

The words hung between us. I'd never worried about anyone evaluating my breasts before. My lovers seemed pleased that I *had* them, but they didn't ever go critical on me. I still wasn't sure why I was offering myself to Sara Jane in this way but I couldn't take it back. I started sweating and felt nervous. What if she didn't like them? What if she laughed at them? Suddenly, a lot was riding on my boobies.

"I'd love to see yours, Em. I'm dying to know what a B looks like." She said it quietly, gently. Very un-Sara Jane.

"Right now?"

"Right now."

I unbuttoned my blouse quickly, unhooked my bra and let my breasts fall free. I watched her face. She beamed with happiness and surprise.

"They're wonderful, Em. Perfect." She stared at them longer than any lover had, sizing them up, studying them. Finally, she turned her big eyes to my face and they looked wet.

"Mine will be scarred," she said quietly, almost the way a child would. Neither of us spoke for a long time.

"I know," I told her.

Before I knew what was happening, Sara Jane reached out and touched my breast, the gentlest touch I'd ever felt, like a butterfly landing on your finger. The contact lasted less than a few seconds, then Sara Jane wrinkled her nose, grinned and scrunched her shoulders as she removed her hand. Though the moment was brief, it seemed to stretch between us soft as taffy.

"You better get your camera, Sara Jane. I don't intend to stand like this forever."

"I don't see why not—you're magnificent. It's in here somewhere." She fumbled through her purse and finally pulled out a small 35 mm, a point-and-shoot variety. A quick flash and it was over. All I could see was a red Sara Jane standing in front of me, camera in hand, all energy and image, all guts and glory.

OPAL

Fall, 1985

It'd been seven weeks and three days since my husband, Walter, last came to my bed and I was fidgety as a cackle of hens when the rooster's stewing for Sunday dinner, as my aunt Pearl used to say. I'd been staring at a frozen turkey breast for five minutes, trying to figure out what to do with it for supper. I spun it around a couple of times, hoping a recipe might pop into my head. But all I could think about was Walter and me. And sex.

Our love life had been going downhill for the last two years until now it looked like it was grinding to a halt completely. At first, I thought the lack of interest was normal, something that happened to people who'd been married a while. Walter and I celebrated our tenth wedding anniversary last year and I knew enough to realize married life was no picnic, but I still wanted Walter as much as ever. But Walter didn't seem to want me—at least not more than once a month. Now, it'd been almost two.

Strange things had been catching my eye. Like advertisements for men's underwear in the Sunday sports section. What normal woman spent the Lord's day with her nose stuck in a newspaper?

It wasn't just pictures that had me worried. My regular activities had taken an unusual turn. When I washed dishes, it was all I could do to keep my mind off the high school football team practicing in the field below my house. Those uniforms squared off the shoulders of even the skinniest boy and I sometimes caught myself wondering what it would be like to slowly unbutton each button of my blouse, then run my fingers across some quarterback's milky chest.

When I was at the sink peeling potatoes, I sometimes found myself in the middle of a steamy soap opera. Instead of Kayla kissing Patch on *Days of Our Lives*, it was me. And I kissed him all over, even on his bad eye. Before I knew what'd happened, the potato bag was empty and I'd peeled enough spuds to feed a platoon.

I looked at the turkey breast in its plastic wrapper, then tucked it under my arm as if it were a football and returned it to the freezer. Turkey wouldn't solve my problem. I sat down at the kitchen table and leafed through an old cookbook, hoping for inspiration.

I didn't know how long I could go on like this. Two months wasn't such a long time, but it seemed longer than a summer drought. It felt like that, too—empty, lifeless. My skin prickled like one touch would burn it redder than a Bigboy tomato. And I wanted to be burned. I wanted to go up in flames.

I flipped through the Joy of Cooking until I came to the section on casseroles. Walter didn't care for them, but I liked the idea of a meal in one dish. Hamburger Stroganoff caught my eye. One pound lean ground beef, can of mushroom soup, cooking wine... .

What I couldn't figure was why my man didn't know I was needy. And why wasn't he? I knew his muscles hurt sometimes, but what about his love muscle? He wasn't dead yet, so how come he didn't seem to want me? I turned it over in my mind until I was dizzy. I sent out every signal I knew—I wiggled when I walked, I smiled and batted my eyes at him, I even reached out to touch his arm sometimes—but he didn't notice a thing.

Could be he'd got himself somebody on the sly. Moon hired a young gal in the accounting department a few months back. Walter told me she was good-looking, but not too friendly. Maybe she'd warmed up some.

Or maybe Walter was sicker than I realized, really sick. I just didn't understand how a muscle ache could rob a man of his desires. He'd been down in his back for some time. Old Doc Murphy told him it was some kind of rheumatism, but Walter was just thirty-three. I couldn't figure why he'd have something like that at his age. Doc Murphy explained it to me, said Walter had "pain drain," that's when a person's hurting all the time. He said to me, "Now Opal, you got to be patient with Walter. This arthritis kinda comes and goes. Don't baby him, but don't expect him to be the man he was in his twenties."

What Doc Murphy didn't seem to understand was that I was only thirty, heading toward my 'sexual peak' just like it said in that Cosmopolitan magazine at the grocery store: *Women Over Thirty Have Everything to Look Forward To—Hot Love in Prime Time.* Why God gave men their primes at eighteen and made women wait until they were thirty-five, I didn't know. I guessed if they hit their primes at the same time, not much civilization would take place.

I kept turning the pages of the cookbook. Eggplant Surprise. I'd be surprised if Walter would put one forkful of eggplant into his mouth. I turned to the next section—Dinner for Two, Meals for the Romantic-At-Heart. Maybe I could try something from this section. Maybe a little Beef Wellington with sour cream mashed potatoes would stir Walter.

Walter was too young to go around acting like an old man. Besides, Walter didn't act sick when the love mood struck him—it just doesn't strike him regular enough.

I turned to the dessert section. Sinful Chocolate Mousse, Better-Than-Sex-Cake. The Million-Dollar-Gold Cake. Raspberry Sorbet... .

That left one thing—Walter didn't love me anymore. When I thought about that possibility, I felt like old biscuit dough—lumpy and cold.

This morning while I fried bacon and whipped some eggs for scrambling, I stood right next to Walter and put my arms around his waist.

"I've got to get ready, woman. Besides, my muscles are acting up. Don't like to be pulled at," he said and pushed me out of the way. I didn't say a word. My mama always told me if you can't say something nice, don't say anything at all. Instead, I turned back to the eggs and stirred in some bits of cheese and onions. Walter sat down, gulped his orange juice and read the newspaper. I fixed a bowl of corn flakes with raisins sprinkled on top and silently shoveled them into my mouth. Walter studied the front page like it was the holy Bible. When he buzzed my cheek on his way out the door, I wiped off the kiss with the back of my hand and my eyes filled up. I couldn't finish my breakfast so I dumped the soggy cereal into the trash and got ready for work.

I wasn't a sex fiend. I was just used to Walter, used to our lovemaking, and I didn't want to get un-used to it. He was still the good man I married, but something was different now, there was something sad and lonely about him. Lots of times, especially in rainy weather, he sat in front of the TV with a heating pad on his back. Yesterday, my heart flip-flopped when he grabbed my hand while I was on my way to the kitchen to fix supper. I just knew he was going to pull me down to him and say, like he does, "Woman, it's been too long. I miss you."

But all he said was "Honey, bring me some ginger ale." He sat there comfy as a snail in its shell. Sometimes I wondered if he saw me at all, or if I'd somehow grown

What You Long For

invisible—a food-and-clothes-fairy that sneaked him what he needed when he wasn't looking.

I slammed the Joy of Cooking shut. We'd have pancakes for supper. Pancakes and sausage. If Walter didn't like it, he could go to the hotel, as Aunt Pearl used to say. I was tired of the way Walter ignored me, tired of feeling sad.

I met Walter eleven years ago at *Pee Dee Pete's*, the big hang-out for single folks in their twenties, the only place in Floyd, South Carolina where a body could cut loose a little. Thursday night was Ladies' Night, when all the women could drink for free until nine.

One Thursday about 9:30, Walter walked in. I spied him out of the corner of my eye, the way I noticed everybody who came through the door. He wasn't very tall, maybe 5'10", but his body was solid and he had a nice swagger—not too cocky, but at ease. I couldn't see his face because it was covered by a big, dark beard. I'd been trying to talk my best friend, Beth Waters, out of getting drunk. Her boyfriend, Ronnie, had walked out on her after two and a half years of living together. And he hadn't paid his half of the rent.

"I shouldn't have let that low-down rascal move in with me. You and Magic Eight were right all along—-I should have slammed the door in his sweet-looking face." Beth slugged down another long swallow of beer.

"Magic Eight's usually right. Scary, huh?" I said, remembering when Beth first met Ronnie and the two of us sat on her bed holding my Magic Eight Ball in our hands, questioning it like it held all the truth we'd ever need. I looked at her, mascara beginning to smudge, her eyes brimmed full of tears. "But you can start over. There's lots of fish in the sea. Next time, you'll hook a good one. " I patted her arm. I've always tried to stand by my friends as long as I could. I didn't believe in living with a man unless you were married to him, but that was just because I came from a long line of Bible-believing folks.

"I'm going to let you wear my lucky necklace," I said as I lifted the gold chain over my head and dropped it into her hand. "This'll bring you good things. It's a little gold angel, see?" I'd worn the charm since seventh grade when my teacher, Miss Clark, gave it to me as a consolation prize when I lost the spelling bee to Maria Simpson on the word a-t-t-a-c-k. I'd spelled a-t-t-I-c- and one of the boys told me the way to tell the difference between a-t-t-a-c-k and what I'd spelled, was to look down my shirt and say real fast, "a-titty-I-see." I'd been so embarrassed that I cried in front of everybody and Miss Clark felt sorry for me so she gave me the angel.

"Oh, Opal, I'll treasure it forever," Beth said with tears in her eyes. She was well on her way to being what my Aunt Pearl used to call 'three sheets in a hurricane.' She kept trying to talk to every man in sight about her troubles. "Hey handsome, come on over here," she'd call whenever a man walked by. It didn't matter what kind of man, either. Short, tall, blond, gray, Beth tried to reach for his arm.

When Walter strolled up to the bar, right past our table, Beth grabbed his sleeve and asked him if he wanted to hear a tale that'd break his heart. Unlike the others, he stopped. I couldn't look at him.

He sat down next to Beth and listened real politely to her story. He told her how pretty she was, that Ronnie was a damned fool. He told her she ought to head on home and sleep it off, then he turned to me.

"Can you get her home okay?" he asked. I got the funniest feeling when I heard his voice. Like I could be myself with him. Like he didn't expect anything but friendliness. That was a rare thing at *PeeDee Pete's*.

"Yeah. Reckon she's had about enough," I said and smiled at him. Walter's brown eyes seemed kind and honest. We got Beth out to my car and Walter told us to be careful. Then, when I was just about ready to pull out of the parking lot, he asked if I'd be back tomorrow night. I told him maybe.

All the next day I studied about Walter. I thought about how gentle he'd been with Beth. How he didn't try to make a pass at her. He'd been careful of her feelings. I also recalled the looks he'd gotten from some of the other women and the slight swagger of his hips when he walked.

Beth wanted me to spend Friday night at her place. She was hung over, so I figured we could rent old movies and I could keep her from brooding about Ronnie. By the time Indiana Jones was over, I was ready for some beer, though Beth was sticking to soda. I drove over to *Pete's* to pick it up and Beth said she'd make some popcorn. I didn't mention that I'd be going to *Pete's* to get it, scared to say that Walter might be waiting for me. I didn't want her to think I had somebody when she'd just lost her Ronnie.

I told her if I wasn't back in a half hour to start the other movie without me. I reminded her that sometimes the traffic could be bad, especially with the cruising teens on Friday nights.

When I walked into *Pete's*, the place was packed. I had to snake my way to the bar, turning sideways, first left, then right. It was impossible not to brush against perfect strangers. I tried to scope out the place to see if I could glimpse Walter. I didn't want to look like I was *looking*.

"Who you lookin fer, Opal?" Pete handed me a beer.

"Nobody. Busy tonight, ain't it?" I swallowed a big gulp of Miller Light and grimaced. I scoured the room again and was just about to give up when I felt a tug on my elbow.

"Glad you made it." Walter had trimmed his beard and looked better than I remembered. He grinned at me.

"I just stopped in for a quick one. Beth and I are watching movies. She just got a VCR." I took another swig and felt the bubbles hit the back of my throat. I could feel a burp coming and the last thing I wanted to do was belch that smelly beer in his face. I turned away.

"Cool. I might splurge and get one with my next paycheck." Walter kept his eyes on me. At least, I thought I could feel them on the back of my head.

"Where you from?" I asked.

"North Carolina, up near Brown's Summit. Went to Guilford Tech and studied automotive mechanics. Thought I'd come to Darlington, you know—see if I could break into the racing business," he said, gazing at me with eyes the color of a spaniel's.

"Have you?" I said, giving him as good a look as he gave me.

"Naw, not yet," he said.

"You got family around here?" I said.

"Don't have much in the way of family." He leaned in, his voice bumping over the words as if they were pebbles in his way. We kept talking, back and forth, eyes locked. We covered everything, like we were long lost friends who'd been reunited after twenty years.

After a couple more beers, he confessed he'd been seeing a woman, a married woman, since he'd moved to Floyd. They'd spent week nights together and he stayed home most weekends because he didn't want to chance being unfaithful to her.

"I thought she really loved me, you know? Then, one night while we were making love, she called me Horace. Now, that wasn't her husband's name and it sure as hell wasn't mine." He touched my hand. "Let's go someplace a little more quiet. Trying to talk in here's like singing in a hail storm." He finished his beer and looked at me.

"Okay. Where?" I said. I didn't have any idea where we might find the luxury of quiet. Not at my place. I still lived with my mom and she'd probably make us play Spades.

"I'll think of something. Let's go."

"I've got to call Beth. I don't want her to worry." I had a twinge of guilt leaving Beth alone, running after Walter when I hardly knew him. But something about him made

What You Long For

me ignore it. Besides, I knew if Beth had the chance, she'd do the same thing.

I followed him in my car. I might have been from Floyd, but at least I knew enough to keep my own transportation handy. You never knew what kind of person you might run into, even in a little dinky place like this.

We drove straight through Main Street and kept going. The night was clear, everything in deep shadow. A full moon cast a pearly glow on the trees. It was summer and I could whiff honeysuckle as we sped down the road. We turned several times, going further and further away from town. We were headed for a part of the county I didn't know as well, the seedy part, full of mobile homes and cotton fields. Finally, Walter pulled into a yard where a very old trailer stood.

I'm not proud of what happened next. Walter took me inside and turned on the lights. We sat on the sofa and talked until I didn't have any more voice. Then we made love.

It's not that I was a virgin or anything. I'd had a few boyfriends before, but not since I'd rededicated my life to Jesus last summer at our church revival. Since then, I'd tried to be without sin as much as possible. But that night with Walter, sin was far from my mind. All I could think about was how he felt, his smooth skin, the dark hair curled on his chest. And I could tell he wasn't afraid. Of all the boys I'd been with, he was the only one who pulled me to him like I belonged there. He tasted right; he even smelled right. I caught the faint odor of sweat underneath the scent of his deodorant and found myself wanting more. That night, I fell impossibly in love with Walter Cooper.

But that was more than ten long years ago. Now things were so bad that when the delivery boy came by today with Walter's pain pills, I found myself smiling and batting my eyes at him like I was in tenth grade. He smiled right back at me, natural as could be.

"I was passing this way. Thought I'd drop the medication by," the fellow said to me, his face turning pink. I didn't say anything and he kept going. "I'm trying to get to know all the regular customers. Mr. 'S' said it was about time I got to know the 'people I serve.'" He grinned at me, his blond hair cut short. It would be scarce by the time he was forty. His eyes were light blue-green with a darker ring at the edge, as if the watery blue would spill all out but for that rim. He wasn't tall, maybe a head taller than me. His hands were small, delicate.

"That's real nice. Mr. Snow's always done right by us. One time my husband was sick with the flu in the dead of winter. Snow let us run a bill and he didn't say a word about it, even though it took us till April to pay it off." I don't know why I told him that. I was so aware of his eyes I couldn't think what to say.

"Small towns. Guess that's why I moved back."

"You from here?" I didn't recognize him. Surely I'd have noticed somebody that handsome around here.

"Don't you know me?"

"No, no I don't," I said.

He seemed to recollect me very well. By now, his grin was big and happy.

"Victor Wall." He stood and waited for some response.

"Oh. Hi, Victor." I smiled and pretended he was someone familiar.

"You still don't remember me, do you? We went to school together—I was a freshman and you were a senior. I had the biggest crush on you." His voice turned gravelly and the way he said it made me realize he was flirting with me.

"Well...that was a long time ago, wasn't it? So, you've come back to good old Floyd. Why?" I swung my foot back and forth like a school girl.

"I worked in Charlotte for a while, but I got enough of the big city. I liked the idea of knowing my 'regulars.'" His

What You Long For

mouth looked dry and I couldn't help wondering how those powdery lips would feel against my skin.

"You married?" I asked.

"Not yet. But I'm on the lookout. Too bad you're already spoken for." He smiled again.

"Too bad." I laughed and took the small bag from his hand, careful not to touch his fingers. We stood a while longer, chatting about the drugstore, the neighbors. He was friendly, even said I looked pretty in my red blouse. And when he smiled, his eyes seemed to grow a shade lighter. He asked me what I did for a living. For a minute, I felt the old embarrassment creep into my mind—I'd never gone past high school and sometimes that bothered me, especially when I was talking to anybody who was educated.

"I work over at the rest home—Shady Pines." It had been a long time since I'd held a man's attention long enough to have a real conversation. At least, a man who still had his teeth and hair, who could walk without a walker.

"Man, I'd hate that."

"I really like it. Working with the old folks… .well, it gives me a head start on death. I know what it looks like and how it smells." I'd never told anyone that before, not even Walter. It seemed silly once I said it out loud. "You probably think I'm crazy." I looked down at my feet and felt a blush creep up my neck.

"Yeah, but a good kind of crazy." He turned, hopped down the steps and got into his truck. After a quick wave, he drove down the driveway.

I suddenly noticed how the first red leaves of October held as many shades as the feathers of a cardinal. The sky grew bigger, bluer. In the few moments I'd talked with Victor, I found a man listening to me, asking me questions about my very own life. There were no aches or pains to discuss, no complaints. There was no remedy for me to search out, no ailment to hear about. For the first time since Walter's back trouble developed, the first time in three long years,

I knew I was alive. I realized how much I missed simple conversation with a man.

The sun shone through the scarlet leaves on the oak and it seemed as if Fall would never really come: the weather during the day was still summer-hot. I stared out the front window, half watching the road for signs of Walter, half wishing that Victor would make another delivery. I reconsidered the pancake supper I'd decided on. Walter loved pork chops and black-eyed peas. Maybe I'd make him some buttermilk biscuits, the way my mama taught me. I felt suddenly kindly toward Walter, him working hard all week at Moon's, even with the hurt in his back, the aching that never seemed to go away. My heart grew tender, but I knew deep inside something about talking to Victor Wall had caused the new feeling, not Walter. It had nothing to do with Walter.

I measured the flour for biscuits into a bowl and cut little bits of butter all over. I was just ready to pour in the buttermilk when the phone rang. I wiped my hands on a paper towel and answered.

"Hey, Walter. I was just fixin' supper." I smiled thinking of him, tender little thoughts. Maybe I could flirt a little with my own husband for a change.

"Good," he said. "I'm starved. What we having?"

"You'll just have to hurry home to see. It's a surprise." I sucked on my finger.

"I'm on my way, baby. Been one hell of a day." His voice was thin.

"Well, then, you need some TLC. That's what we'll have for dessert—Tender Loving Cake." I couldn't believe I talked so bold, but seeing Victor earlier that day reminded me that I was, indeed, a woman.

"Aw, baby, I'm tired. Besides, the Clemson game's on tonight. I been looking forward to it. Hold that thought for the weekend, okay?"

"That's fine, Walter, just fine." I hung up before I could stop myself. I crossed over to where I'd been making biscuits and dumped the contents of the bowl into the garbage. I looked in the freezer, found a large cheese pizza, opened the flimsy box and tossed the crust onto a cookie sheet, threw it like a Frisbee. The oven rack rang like a church bell as the pan hit it. I didn't care. I marched into the living room, flung myself onto the couch and stared into the open door of our woodstove. I tossed in some logs, lit a fire and watched the flames flicker and burn. My face was hot and I felt as if I could run the hundred yard dash in record time. After a minute, though, I made myself get calm with a few deep breaths. I didn't want to be so mad at Walter. I didn't want to perk up at the thought of football players and pharmacists. I wanted things to be like they used to be.

Things weren't always like they were now between Walter and me. Time was when I'd be walking through the den, my arms loaded down with laundry, Walter'd grab at me, pull me on his lap. Dirty clothes would fall like tumble-down leaves as Walter kissed my neck, his fingers taking a slow stroll along the inside of my legs. I could feel his shoulders work while his hands made little miracles. Soon, he'd be on top of me, inside me, his arms all around me and we'd rock the cradle of love, like Aunt Pearl used to say. Every time that sweet, undeniable shudder would start deep in my belly, Walter would tremble, too, and grunt, "Opal, honey." After, Walter would tease me about 'screaming like a crazy woman', but I didn't remember making a sound.

All marriages went through dry spells—at least that was what the preacher said in a recent sermon. What he didn't say was how low-down you'd feel when you were in the middle of one. When I got to feeling bad like this, I tried to do what my daddy always told me: Count my blessings. I had a warm, dry place to stay; too much food—kept me plump like a banty hen. I had a steady job working with people I cared about. I hadn't been blessed with children but I had a friend who was closer than a sister. Considering these things made me feel better sometimes. What I needed real help with, though, was the desires of the flesh.

I'd read where nuns and other religious folks tried to beat out their fleshly cravings with sticks and such, like that preacher I read about back in high school who punished himself for having a fling with that woman who had to wear the big red 'A.' I used to feel so sorry for her, all ruined and her ruination standing right in front of her clean and pure on the outside, but filled with black sin on the inside like a piece of rotten fruit.

Hiding in the closet to whip yourself didn't sound too reasonable to me. And I didn't want the Lord to take away my hunger because He might think I meant to take it away for good. I wanted to be ready when the iron got hot. But I'd just as soon quit looking at boys on the football field and getting trembly inside.

Or thinking about Victor Wall.

I realized I'd forgotten to turn the oven on, so I returned to the kitchen, removed the still-frozen pizza and twisted the thermostat to 400 degrees. I set the pizza on the counter and thought about Walter and his Clemson game. Everything suddenly seemed hot. I slammed out the backdoor into the crisp evening air and stomped to the persimmon tree. A few pieces of fruit dotted the ground, bright orange balls of slime. I picked up a handful and threw them into the woods as hard as I could. I kept throwing them, one after the other, until my heartbeat finally slowed. Then a thought came to me like a voice from the persimmon tree itself.

Things are going to change around here. That's what the voice said. Things are going to change.

THE SWING

Bascom leans toward the swing, pushes his knotty hands against the bottom board and shoves gently. The wooden slats need painting and Bascom notices the dark green curls breaking off in his fingers. He sighs and decides he'll get to the task in the fall when the air nips at him with cold, not like the oppressive summer heat that sags in on him today. He's never enjoyed August, the way stillness lies in the atmosphere, heavy and full like the belly of a pregnant dog. He feels the pressure of it in his chest, the difficult breath, the sharp little stings against his ribcage.

He won't think of that now. Instead, he'll keep his eyes on the little one in the swing, his Butterball, his granddaughter, Janey. He notices how her nervous hands have stopped their flight now that she's in the swing. And she's no longer mumbling crazy gibberish to herself. Her clear blue eyes are still vacant, a lost look that he can barely stand, but at least she's not slinging her tiny fingers against the air, flailing at whatever she imagines is there.

Swinging always affects her this way. The slow back and forth motion calms her like nothing else can. Now Bascom knows to take her from the womenfolk in the kitchen when he hears their voices go up a notch. He senses Janey's getting into something, fingers in the brown sugar, tongue licking up spills from the table. And he can tell she needs to step out to the front porch with him, crawl into the swing and fly away from everything.

That's how he likes to think of it. He takes her up into the cloudless sky, up and away from whatever troubles her when she's earthbound. She's only four years old, but her mind's agitated in a way no one understands. He offers her the comfort of air and sky, and though the weather is hot, the movement of the swing cools her a little. He imagines Janey's in a rocket ship and he's blasting her off to heaven where the hand of God will touch her and her mind will clear the way a foggy mirror does when you press your finger against the glass. He hopes it will work like that some day for his Janey.

She's small for her age. Her hair is wavy, the honey-color of tall meadow grass in autumn. She has delicate features like her mother's. Virginia, his middle child, always his favorite, is like the shadow of this golden girl. Virginia's hair is black, like his own mother's had been.

And Virginia is beautiful. He hates to admit it, but her loveliness causes him to feel a rare closeness to her. And now, her tragedy, giving birth to this child who will never be normal, little Janey, this misery confirms Virginia in the most special place of his heart.

"Sing, Gwandaddy." Janey's voice startles him. When she speaks, she sounds the way a small bird might sound if it could talk. Janey doesn't communicate very often and she runs over her words so quickly that she's difficult to understand. The womenfolk sometimes lose patience with her, but Bascom doesn't. He knows what it's like to be misunderstood. Fifteen years ago, he lost most of his jaw, half his tongue and all his teeth to cancer. It took a long time for him to make himself clear to people and he still remembers the barely disguised looks of impatience from his wife, Estelle. Even now, he works to shape his words and when he meets a stranger, he must repeat what he says until the new person becomes used to his halting speech.

"Okay, Butterball. How about Camptown Racetrack?" It's one of her favorites.

"Doo-dah? Yes. Sing Doo-dah?" She won't look at him when she talks. Instead, she stares at her hands which she holds up in front of her face, one hand on top of the other. He can't manage all the words to the verses so he hums a little, then sings a bit, always careful to say the doo-dah part at the right time. She joins him. For a few minutes, everything seems normal. He wants this moment to last, so he keeps pushing the swing though his arms are starting to ache. He's used to the pull of his muscles, the tightening, and he keeps the motion steady and slow. He's developed this technique over the last couple of years and finds that he can keep going longer with the movements calculated and precise.

After a while they fall silent. Bascom replays the past and he wonders where Janey's mind goes. He imagines unknown worlds peopled by phantoms and mysterious beings. And he hopes Janey isn't afraid, prays her daydreams are good ones.

Bascom recalls when Virginia herself was a girl. It seems such a long time ago now and he realizes he's smiling at the memory. Virginia caused a stir wherever they went, her raven hair and pale green eyes, the full lips and her sweet expression.

And he remembers Virginia calling them late one night in tears, her voice choking over the words.

"There's something wrong with Janey. Oh, Daddy..." He could swear the phone shook with her sobbing. And there wasn't a thing he could say to comfort her, nothing he could do. The one time she'd turned to him, really needed him, and he was just an old man marked by disease.

"We'll help, Virginia. We've got our savings." He'd tried to comfort her but he knew his words were nothing.

There was silence on the other end and then her husband's voice, explaining that they were doing everything the doctor suggested, there wasn't much really they could do right now. It was the only time Bascom has ever heard Virginia cry about Janey. She keeps her tears hidden from him, tucks them away somewhere deep and private. How he wishes he could wipe them away. What he wouldn't give to fix everything.

He shakes his head, tired out by the dreary thoughts. Janey is watching him, not directly, but with her head down and her eyes cut upwards, a sly, sneaky look. She's like a little imp. He's glad she looks normal. She's cute, though nothing like as pretty as Virginia was. Virginia is still lovely, though now her eyes hold a sadness that gives depth to her beauty, a deepening of the spirit she didn't have before. Sometimes Bascom catches a glimpse of grief as it flashes across her features and she is so beautiful that his heart clinches up in his chest. She's like the paintings he's seen of the Madonna. She has those same sorrowful eyes that seem to know the future and all its heartbreak.

His breathing becomes harder and he's not sure whether it's from the exertion of pushing Janey or whether it's the usual ball of despair he sometimes feels when he's with the child. He takes a quick glance at his watch, careful not to break his rhythm. Almost noon. He's been at it for two hours and Janey shows no sign of boredom. She never signals for him to stop. He knows she doesn't want to return to this world and he doesn't blame her. He's not crazy about it either.

Some days, he wants to linger on the porch, just the two of them. He longs to wrap Janey in his skinny arms, brown and freckled from his long years in the sun, and whisper to her that everything will be all right. But he doesn't know that and he shies away from considering the future, both for him and for little Janey. In seventy-four years, he's known enough of despair and long ago ceased his questions. Now, he focuses on trusting God, the one thing he hopes is true.

He hears his wife's quick step and the opening of the screen door.

"Bascom, almost lunch time. You been out here all morning." Estelle's voice is sharp, though he understands that she doesn't mean anything by it. It has become her way.

"I reckon we're about ready." The child hums more of their song.

"Janey, wash your hands and don't forget to use soap. Granddaddy will help you. We got a good lunch so hurry up." Estelle disappears back into the shade of the house and Ernest pulls the swing to a stop.

"Come on, Butterball, time to eat." Janey makes no move to get off the swing, so he scoops her into his arms and lifts her down. His big gnarly hand envelopes her tiny one and together they walk into the cool parlor, each silent, each remembering the feel of the swing, the easy flight into the summer air.

Author's Gratitude

I'd like to thank M. Scott Douglass for the contribution Main Street Rag continues to make to the literary world and for his indefatigable poetic spirit and courage as a publisher; his able assistants Megan Kohn and S. Craig Renfroe, Jr. for their hard work; my writing friends, Kathryn Lovatt, Kathryn Milam, Sandra Redding, and Isabel Zuber for their honest critiques of my work—their help has been invaluable; to Fred Chappell, Becky Gould Gibson and Julianna Baggott for their examples of how to live the writing life with grace and generosity; to Clyde Edgerton, Philip Gerard, Rebecca Lee, Wendy Brenner and Paul Wilkes for what they taught me about narrative; to my sons, Michael, Jason and Adam, for teaching me to stretch beyond my limits; to Emily for her faith in my work; to Kristi for her love of reading; to my three grandchildren, Virginia, Bela and Langston for the joy you bring me; to Frank, for your loyalty and love.